San Francisco

Story

ALAN MINDELL

MILFORD HOUSE
an imprint of Sunbury Press, Inc.
Mechanicsburg, PA USA

MILFORD HOUSE

an imprint of Sunbury Press, Inc.
Mechanicsburg, PA USA

For information about special discounts for bulk purchases, please contact Sunbury Press Orders Dept. at (855) 338-8359 or orders@sunburypress.com.

To request one of our authors for speaking engagements or book signings, please contact Sunbury Press Publicity Dept. at publicity@sunburypress.com.

FIRST MILFORD HOUSE PRESS EDITION: December 2020

Set in Adobe Garamond | Interior design by Crystal Devine | Cover by Terry Kennedy | Edited by Lawrence Knorr.

Publisher's Cataloging-in-Publication Data
Names: Mindell, Alan, author.
Title: San Francisco story / Alan Mindell.
Description: First trade paperback edition. | Mechanicsburg, PA : Milford House Press, 2020.
Summary: A sex addict and a crack addict become romantically evolved and then try to recover in 1980s San Francisco.
Identifiers: ISBN : 978-620064-56-6 (softcover).
Subjects: FICTION / Romance / Historical / 20th Century | FICTION / Urban & Street Lit | FICTION / Psychological.

Product of the United States of America
0 1 1 2 3 5 8 13 21 34 55

Continue the Enlightenment!

Other books written by Alan Mindell
Published by Sunbury Press

The Closer

The B Team

PART I

Chapter One

I was having trouble falling asleep. It was Saturday night, and Stacy, my older sister, had gone to a dance at our high school. I expected her to wake me when she got back, and want to tell me about all the boys she'd danced with.

"You could have danced with some of them too, Tara," she would remind me.

But there was something else keeping me awake. I was thinking about Dad, wondering how he was doing. For some reason, for the first time since he'd left home more than six months earlier, I was afraid that he'd also left town. I was afraid, too, that he wouldn't be coming back.

I had no idea where he'd gone. I thought maybe he'd left the state or even the country. But where he'd gone didn't seem so important. No, what mattered much more to me was that he was no longer living here at home, and I hadn't seen him since he left, and there seemed little chance that I would see him again soon.

⚬⟨◉⟩⚬

It was nearly midnight when Daniel Stanton left the restaurant. Knowing that sleep would be difficult, he decided against returning to the downtown San Francisco motel room he'd rented about two hours before, following his four-hundred-mile drive from Los Angeles. He needed time to unwind, plus the vague pain in the pit of his stomach suggested that the meal he'd just finished didn't agree with him. Maybe a walk and some fresh air would help.

A horde of oncoming pedestrians was his first obstacle, which he barely managed to sidestep. Dressy, Saturday night attire prevailed, rendering his rumpled road clothing out of place, adding to his discomfort. In addition, everyone else seemed jovial, much different than his somber mood.

Where did all these people come from? Had they been there on his way to the restaurant, he'd have gone elsewhere. He rubbed his cheek, seeking an explanation, then remembered noticing several of the passersby carrying theater programs. Nearby Union Square playhouses must have just let out.

As he headed west, he had to dodge another approaching horde. Hoping to avoid further congestion, he turned south toward Market Street, maybe half a mile away. Numbers began to dwindle. Almost in triumph, he took several deep breaths of fresh air.

A chilly late-February wind blew various papers and other assorted debris across his path. Fortunately, he'd worn his heavy brown coat, and he pulled it tight around his neck. He could feel his tall slim figure grow stiff from the cold. Or maybe it was from tension, plus the ache in his stomach.

As he continued south, even in the dark, he could tell that buildings were decayed, and their outer walls were covered with graffiti. Broken glass, beer cans, and banana peels littered the sidewalk. Someone—coatless and wearing a tattered white T-shirt—accosted him, muttering something, no doubt about drugs. Daniel slipped past him and kept going.

At a street corner, he came upon a woman in a skin-tight gray pantsuit and matching heels. She offered him an open-mouthed grin. Her rotted teeth and the reek of alcohol on her breath prompted him to move on. But not before depositing a few coins into the outstretched hand of an old guy motoring slowly by in a wheelchair.

A tall woman, dressed in black, stood beside the entrance to a hotel. As he passed her, he was surprised that she appeared both younger and more appealing than the neighborhood would imply, though the shadowy light made verification difficult. When she took a cigarette from a very large purse, he saw his chance for a closer look.

"Use a light?" he mumbled, approaching her while managing to dig out a matchbook from a pants pocket.

"Excuse me?" she replied without looking up from her purse.

"Can you use a light?"

"I have my own," she hissed, removing a lighter.

"Sorry for the intrusion."

While turning to leave, he glanced at her again. No question, she looked even better up close. Her hair, cut short, was as dark as her outfit. She wore a low-cut blouse, which offered a glimpse of undergarment beneath. Above spiked heels, she had on slacks, so he couldn't see her legs. But he imagined them long and shapely like the rest of her figure, sending a wave throughout his body.

"You're not a cop?" she muttered, lighting her cigarette.

"Hardly," he answered, pleased that she had interrupted his departure.

"Prove it."

"How?"

"Show me your dick."

"What did you say?"

"You heard me," she declared. "Show me your dick."

"Here?"

"Now. Or don't waste my time."

"How do I know *you're* not a cop?" he managed.

"You don't . . . Now show or go."

"Can I move over there?" he asked, pointing to a dark area away from the slightly illuminated hotel entrance.

"What're you afraid of?" She took a long drag from the cigarette. "You think anyone 'round here gives a shit?"

She had a point. Still, he hesitated. He really should leave. With all his trouble in recent months, this made no sense. Yet his gaze swept over her figure again. The familiar wave passed through him once more. He looked up and down the street, then edged away from the hotel entrance, toward the dark spot. Again he glanced in both directions. No one was around. After pausing for another deep breath, he unzipped his pants. He slid out the end of his penis into the evening chill.

"All the way out," she directed.

He took another look, both up and down the street. The wind rustled some papers nearby, startling him briefly. Shrugging, he inched his exposed member farther out of his pants.

"You're making a big deal over nothing," she mocked, nodding at his dick.

"Very funny."

"Maybe offer you a cut rate. Thing that tiny."

Her ensuing cackle emphasized how far from reality he had slipped. He knew he should leave. Zip up his pants and get the hell out of there.

"Follow me," she instructed.

"Where to?"

"Follow me," she repeated more insistently.

She abruptly strutted away from him, directly into the street. On the other side, she marched along the sidewalk. He zipped up his pants and, after another glance up and down the street, slowly began to trace her steps. Someone wearing a stocking cap yelled to her from across the street, but she ignored him.

He followed well behind her for three blocks. When he eventually caught up, she was standing in front of another hotel. She moved to the entrance and pressed a buzzer. A car passed, and the driver honked its horn loudly, then waved. Her only reaction was to flip her cigarette toward the gutter.

She pressed the buzzer a second time, impatiently. Finally, there was the sound of a reply buzzer, and she pulled the door open. Daniel followed her into a tiny lobby, large enough for only a stained brown couch. One of the walls had a hole in it, with corroded wiring visible. They went to a caged enclosure, where a thin dark man, probably Middle Eastern, stared at an ancient black-and-white television. A large calendar missing part of the seven in the current year, 1987, was attached to the wall behind him.

"Nice place," Daniel commented dryly after detecting the presence of a stale odor, like dried sweat.

"Shut up and give him ten bucks," she directed.

He obeyed, and the guy waved them on without even looking up from the TV. They climbed three flights of stairs. Because there was little lighting, Daniel stumbled twice and nearly fell. He was a little relieved when she didn't ridicule him for his clumsiness.

A long narrow hallway with frayed carpeting met them at the top step. Their room was close, and she took out a key from her purse. As she unlocked the door, he heard a different one slam nearby. A guy with a grim expression rushed past, toward the stairway.

Daniel knew he should follow him, get the hell out of this sordid place. Why ask for trouble his very first night in San Francisco? His stomach still ached, reminding him that his purpose in not returning to his motel room right after the restaurant had been to get some fresh air, and there certainly wasn't any around here. The walk back to the motel might help. But she touched his arm at that moment and guided him into a tiny room.

A single flickering overhead light was the sole illumination. A small filthy throw rug near the door was the only covering for the cement floor. Furnishings numbered two—a lumpy bed and a chair with a broken leg. There was no television or phone. Nor was a closet present, or even a bathroom, which might soon become an urgent deficiency. He heard laughter penetrating the thin walls, evidently from next door.

"Luxurious," he appraised.

"Shut up and take off your pants. Right now."

"We renting this place by the minute?"

"One minute. Exactly how long you got to take off your pants."

A wayward mattress spring poked his butt when he sat down on the bed to remove his shoes. He got up and pulled off his pants, dropping them on the broken-legged chair. He thought he caught her smirking at his multi-colored boxers. Despite keeping his socks on, he could feel the cold from the cement floor on his feet. More laughter came through the walls. The same smell from the lobby, like dried sweat, was very apparent.

"Now what?" he inquired.

"Money on the bed."

"How much?"

"Use your imagination."

He got his wallet from a pants pocket, took out a fifty dollar bill, and put it on the bed.

"You're not very imaginative," she scolded, scooping it up and putting it into her purse. "You're insulting me."

"What if that's all I've got?"

"Not my problem. And you can leave any time you want."

He took another fifty from his wallet and tossed it onto the bed. She grabbed it but continued to look angry. She stood directly in front of him, hands on hips, presenting him another inviting view of undergarment beneath her low-cut blouse. Again a wave ran through him. One more fifty reached the bed. She took it and, along with the second fifty, dropped it into her purse.

"Now your shorts," she ordered.

"When do you undress?"

"When I'm ready."

While removing his shorts, he grinned sheepishly as she eyed him. She nodded toward his coat and shirt. He took them off, placing them and his shorts on top of his pants, even though he was concerned the chair might collapse from the weight. Despite the room being much warmer than outside, he began to feel cold without his clothes on.

She unbuttoned her blouse, allowing him a clear view of a black brassiere. She stepped over to him and flicked his dick with her index finger. Opening her purse again, she slipped out two pairs of steel handcuffs.

"You're a cop," he stammered.

"Relax, dummy. You think cops unbutton their blouses in front of idiots like you?"

"Then why the cuffs?"

"You're pretty stupid, aren't you? Now slide up to the top of the bed."

"This isn't what I'm paying for."

"You have no idea what you're paying for. And no one's begging you to stay."

She chose that moment to remove her unbuttoned blouse and toss it onto the bed. Next came her spiked heels and slacks. She still wore only black—panties and bra. Her legs were long and sleek, as he'd imagined. He envisioned her taking off her underwear and felt his dick expand. Sure, the handcuffs might inhibit him a little, but the idea of her wrapping those long legs around him was overwhelming. Regardless of this miserable environment. Regardless of any possible danger.

"Staying or leaving?" she asked impatiently.

"Staying," he conceded.

"Then slide up to the top of the bed."

Shrugging, he relented. As she skillfully cuffed his wrists to metal bedposts behind him, she allowed her body to brush against his. He watched her chest heave while she breathed throatily. After testing to make sure he was securely tied, she stepped back away from him.

"Now what?" he quizzed, his eagerness a little guarded.

"Guess."

"I can't."

"You're more stupid than I thought."

Methodically, she put on her slacks. She casually slipped on her heels. He didn't speak right away. Finally, when she started to button her blouse, he had to say something.

"You're not leaving, are you?"

"You're not just stupid, are you?" she mimicked. "You're a moron."

Finished buttoning her blouse, she removed a pocket mirror and brush from her purse and admired herself while combing her hair. Next, she went to his wallet and took out the rest of his money. He felt his anger grow.

"You're not leaving me like this!" he blurted.

"What do you think I'm doing?"

"Handcuffed, no money, no pants!" he continued, disregarding her question.

"You can have your pants."

She forcefully tipped over the chair, scattering his clothing onto the floor. She grabbed his pants and chucked them at him, hitting him in the face, startling him. She reached deep into her purse as if searching for something hard to find. He sensed that he should be in no hurry to learn what it was.

"A little present," she announced, flashing a key and pointing to the cuffs, then flipping the key against the wall farthest from the bed.

"Bitch."

"Now, don't be nasty," she chided. "Last jerk, I tossed the key right out the window. Heard they had to chainsaw him loose. Wish I could've been there to watch. Him lying there naked. Just like you."

She cackled as she had outside. Daniel, certainly aware of his nakedness, grimaced without uttering a word. A loud burst of laughter, almost as though orchestrated, came through the walls. She moved to the door and paused.

"Oh," she went on, snickering, "and I kicked him in the nuts too."

He grimaced again.

"Behaved himself after that," she laughed.

"How long I have to stay here like this?"

"Stay as long as you like," she chuckled. "Make yourself comfortable."

"You know what I mean."

"Some mornings, they send up a maid. Hope she likes you better than I did."

"What if I yell the second you leave?" His anger had mounted again, although probably more from his helplessness and the fact that he'd allowed himself to get into this predicament than any sadism on her part.

"Go ahead," she encouraged. "Yell all you want. Yell right now."

She stepped over beside him and slapped his face. Then she punched him in the stomach. Neither act, especially the latter, helped his queasiness. In his position, wrists clasped behind him, all he could manage was a pathetic groan.

"Go ahead," she repeated. "Yell. Scream . . . Next punch is six inches lower, and they call you Squeaky rest of your life."

He didn't reply. Fear had replaced anger. He felt himself beginning to shiver. Once more, she went to the door and paused.

"Oh," she said, "to let you know . . . I've still got the room key. And some my pals'd just love to come up here and beat the crap out of a piece of shit like you."

Again, realizing he'd only make things worse, he didn't reply.

"Nighty night," she laughed. "Don't let the bed bugs bite."

She turned off the flickering overhead light and left, slamming the door loudly behind her.

⁂

This was the second time in recent months that Daniel Stanton had been handcuffed. The previous incident occurred late on a warm night, near his home in L.A. Then too, a dark-haired woman, dressed in black, was the attraction.

"What'll it be?" she had asked, leaning against the passenger door of his stationary, late-model, tan Buick, after he'd flagged her down while she walked on a dark side street.

"What're you offering?" he replied, catching a glimpse of black undergarment beneath her top.

"What're you after?" she winked. "Cost you at least fifty bucks. Got that much?"

"Sure."

"Turn the corner," she said, pointing on ahead. "Wait for me there."

As he drove forward expectantly, he watched her image in his rear-view mirror to make sure she followed. When he slowly turned right at the corner, she was only a few steps behind. He parked and put out his headlights. No sign of her in the mirror. He sensed trouble. Because he'd concentrated so much on the mirror, he didn't become aware until it was too late that a car had approached in front of him and blocked any possible escape.

"Get out, pal," a large, casually dressed man commanded while leaning against the same passenger door the woman, still not in view, leaned against moments earlier.

"Hands where we can see 'em," a second guy instructed from the window next to Daniel.

As Daniel got out, he caught the reflection of handcuffs and a police badge in the dim light. He heard the click of his wrists being locked behind him. The two men herded him to another car in a nearby parking lot, where they frisked him, fingerprinted him, snapped his picture, removed his wallet from a pants pocket, examined his driver's license, and took all his cash.

"Third time's the charm, buddy," another guy, also dressed casually, told him inside the car while looking at a computer printout.

"What?" Daniel asked.

"You know what . . . Soliciting an undercover officer. Third offense."

"So, you guys are all cops."

"Duh," the cop mocked. "Call us The Three Musketeers. Banding together to fight the dreaded spread of AIDS."

"All I did was say I had fifty bucks," Daniel attempted in his most conciliatory tone, of course realizing he'd stupidly fallen into their trap.

"Fifty bucks you don't have anymore," the cop dryly retorted.

Because it was too late to contact someone to arrange bail, Daniel had spent that night in jail. Despite being confined to merely a detention cell, private and away from sentenced inmates, he didn't sleep all night. And he got enough of a whiff of prison life to know that he wanted no part of it.

Fortunately, he could afford a good attorney. With connections to work out a plea bargain well before his case went to trial. Community service plus a very stiff fine. No jail time at least, other than that one night.

Unfortunately, he couldn't keep all this from his wife. Daniel proposed counseling and a second honeymoon to redeem himself, but when it came out that this wasn't his first offense and there was plenty of evidence that his involvement in this sort of activity was far from infrequent, she declined. Their twenty-two-year marriage was over. She filed for divorce, and it became final only days before he left for San Francisco.

Based on his current position—manacled to a bedpost in this rundown hotel—she'd made the right decision.

᠁

For nearly twenty years, from the late 1960s until the middle of the prior year, 1986, Daniel Stanton spent most nights in a pleasant Los Angeles neighborhood with his wife and his two currently high-school-aged daughters. Flowers, trees, and shrubbery adorned the front and back-yards of their spacious four-bedroom home. He even had his office-den, featuring a computer, television, and small library.

None of this was available to him any longer. Lying there on that lumpy bed, as he had for hours now, naked and cold, he couldn't avoid mourning his loss. Nor contrasting then with now. How could he have slipped so far?

His head ached from the woman's slap. His stomach hurt where she'd punched him. Or maybe from his earlier meal. Whichever, he felt like vomiting. If only the room had a bathroom, and if only he could get up off the bed to use it.

Intermittently, he had tried to sleep. Not a chance, with his aching head and stomach. With his wrists cuffed and sporadic laughter still coming through the walls. With the odor of dried sweat so pungent. Apparently, he'd lie awake all night, like he had that time in jail.

And what about when morning finally came? Would there be someone to free him? Did this place really have a maid, as the woman suggested? Not likely, based on what he'd seen here so far.

What if he had to spend more than one night chained to this bed? No food, no water. Unable to use a bathroom even if there was one here to use. Maybe that was his fate—to die in his own puke or shit.

A knock at the door. No audible footsteps from the hallway, no other warning, just a knock. Had she returned? Or had she dispatched some of her pals like she'd threatened—to beat the crap out of him? Or was it the knock of a rescuer?

"Who's there?" Daniel ventured cautiously.

"Sorry, man," a male voice answered. "Wrong room, wrong floor."

"Wait," Daniel called out hopefully, thinking that, rather than danger, this might be help. "I could use a hand."

"Sorry, man. Wrong room. Wrong floor."

"Try the door. Or go get the desk clerk."

Now Daniel did hear footsteps in the hallway, trailing away from the door. Was the guy heading off to get the desk clerk, as he'd requested?

Daniel held his breath. Another knock, coming from across the hall, followed by a pause.

"Sorry, man," the guy repeated. "Wrong room. Wrong floor."

Unfortunately, Daniel's question had been answered. The guy probably wasn't capable of locating the desk clerk, let alone leading him up three flights of stairs to the correct room. All Daniel got from their brief exchange was a little more frustrated and weary.

Once more, he tried to sleep. This time his own fantasy kept him awake. He imagined the woman returning, not to harm him, but to provide satisfaction. She stood over him, wearing only her black bra and panties. She was so close that he could reach out and touch her long sleek legs. She leaned over him and, like much earlier, allowed her body to brush against his. He felt his dick grow hard.

Abruptly, he ended the fantasy. He knew very well that it would be solely to deliver more pain and torment if she returned. While lying in jail that night, he'd imagined the undercover policewoman returning too. Right there to his cell. She'd presented him another glimpse of black undergarment beneath her top.

He shook his head vigorously at the memory. At the idea of a policewoman, no less, coming to his cell to pleasure him. Where was his mind? No wonder he'd lost his home and family.

Virtually on cue, his thoughts spun back to his last ten years or so in L.A. In particular, to all the things he used to do there, which ultimately led to this, his lying helplessly in a sordid hotel room. His numerous visits to massage parlors, bondage and discipline houses, taxi dance clubs, and lingerie shops. Places which were often no more than poorly disguised fronts for prostitution. He also often patronized escort services, which were even less clandestine. And, of course, if all else failed, there were always the streets. How he'd managed to keep all this from his wife for most of those ten years was pretty much a miracle.

Again he shook his head vigorously. He couldn't believe all he used to do in L.A. And what a moron he was—as the woman had called him—for winding up here tonight. He even recalled a TV comedy sitcom in which one of the main characters ended up exactly where he was now.

Except he, Daniel, wasn't laughing. With all his stupidity, did he really deserve any better than to die here in his own puke and shit?

Sunlight began to enter the room through the window. Morning had finally arrived, and evidently, it would be a nice day outside, a prospect that currently seemed irrelevant. Maybe the sun had a calming effect on him, though, because he did manage to doze off. Only to be awakened almost immediately by a nearby whirring garbage truck.

⋅❦⋅

"Staying or leaving?" a male voice boomed out from the hallway, accompanied by a loud knock at the door, waking Daniel after he'd finally fallen asleep again. Instinctively, he glanced up at his wrists, still attached to the bedposts. Another glance, this one at his body, confirmed that his naked state hadn't changed.

"You staying another night?" the voice shouted once more, impatiently.

"You the desk clerk?" Daniel replied warily.

"What?"

"You the desk clerk?"

"Plus everything else 'round here."

"You got a key?" Daniel questioned, still wary.

"Sure."

"Can you come in?"

"Hey pal," the voice retorted with a warning tone, no lower in volume. "No weird shit."

Had he been in better humor, Daniel might have laughed at the idea that he could do anything at all, weird or otherwise. As it was, he didn't reply, realizing that if the desk clerk came in, he could very well interpret his, Daniel's, position as no better than weird. When Daniel heard the key in the lock, he recalled the woman's threat and immediately became concerned that he was opening himself up to more trouble. A burly black guy entered the room. With jowly cheeks, a swollen lip, and a gash on his forehead, he looked nothing like the thin desk clerk of the prior night.

"No, not again!" he exclaimed loudly.

Daniel didn't know how to respond, so he didn't. The man had a mean look on his face, and Daniel assumed that he'd been in a fight and very likely would welcome another. Again he recalled the woman's threat.

"She leave the key?" the guy queried.

Still not believing that he wasn't about to be pummeled, Daniel cautiously nodded toward the wall against which the woman had flipped the key to the handcuffs. The man went over to the wall and bent over to look for it. The laughter coming through the walls, which had finally stopped for an hour or two, started up again. Daniel became worried that the guy wouldn't find the key, especially when he started shaking his head. The laughter grew louder as if signaling that they were wasting their time trying to locate the key. Finally, the man fingered it and lifted it to show him. Apparently, there'd be no chainsaws in Daniel's immediate future.

"Damn night guy," the man muttered. "Sits in front of that dumb TV all the time. Told him dozen times not to rent to her."

Instead of fretting over chainsaws, Daniel could now agonize about his nakedness staring the guy in the face. As he stood over Daniel, the man's expression was far short of congenial while he tried to unlock the cuffs. Because of what looked to be several broken fingers, no doubt sustained in past altercations, he had difficulty fitting the key into the lock. Daniel held his breath, visions of chainsaws recurring. Finally, he welcomed the clicking sounds of the cuffs coming loose. Almost in celebration, he raised his arms and tried to shake the numbness from them.

"Had to call an ambulance for the last cat," the guy went on. "Blood all over the place. 'Fraid he might croak on me."

"Guess I was lucky," Daniel commented without much conviction.

"Yeah," the man winked. "She must've liked you."

"Sure," Daniel responded dryly, his tone self-mocking. "She must've liked me."

Feeling was returning to his arms and his wrists and hands also. He managed to partially cover himself with his pants, which had lain beside him on the bed all night after she'd chucked them at him. He struggled up and over to the chair for the rest of his clothes.

"Give you some money," he offered, grateful to his rescuer, especially for not mentioning his nakedness. "But she took it all."

"She always does."

"I'll bring you some later."

"Don't bother. Do yourself a favor . . . Stay away from here. And from her."

Daniel shrugged.

"You never answered my question," the guy proceeded.

"Which one?"

"The one about whether you're gonna ignore my advice," the guy laughed. "And stay another night."

"Only if I can get your penthouse suite," Daniel laughed too, showing lightness for the first time during their entire exchange.

"Sorry," the man winked while heading for the door. "Already booked for tonight."

He left, and Daniel finished dressing. His departure from the room was accompanied by one more round of laughter through the walls. Despite his eagerness to get out of the hotel once and for all, he was relieved to find a community bathroom down the hall. After stopping there, he descended the stairs, practically running into the same guy who had rushed past them the prior night while the woman unlocked their room door. The same grim expression was on his face.

When Daniel finally got outside, he found clouds and drizzle. He'd been wrong in anticipating a nice day.

Chapter Two

Daniel Stanton was again awakened by a loud knock at the door. He initially thought, because his wrists and arms hurt, that he'd only dreamed he'd escaped the dismal hotel room. Then he saw that he had pajamas on, and his suitcases and other possessions were in a corner of his motel room.

"Maid," a female voice announced.

"What?" he uttered, once more confused, recalling the woman in black's reference to a maid.

"Maid," she repeated. "To clean your room. I'm off in half an hour."

"What time is it?"

"Four."

His confusion began to lift. Struggling out of bed and over to the door, he remembered trudging the few blocks back to his motel that morning. He'd gone to the office to hold his room another night and to get a cash advance from his credit card. Although the desk clerk looked at him suspiciously, he'd granted both requests. After that, Daniel returned to his room, hanging the "do not disturb" sign outside his door before crashing into bed.

"Come in," he told the maid, an unusually tall woman after he unlocked the door.

"Sorry, sir. Not with you in the room. Motel policy."

He dressed quickly. He barely took time to brush his teeth and run a comb through his gray hair. A glance in the bathroom mirror surprised him that he didn't look worse after what he'd been through. His thin face with high cheekbones and large nose was neither red nor swollen from her slap, and his blue eyes even appeared to have a slight glow. No doubt sleeping all day had agreed with him.

Once outside, he flipped over the "do not disturb" sign. Like that morning, it was drizzling, so he went to his car in the motel parking lot and took out an umbrella. He deliberately headed off in the opposite direction from where he'd wound up last night, toward Union Square. As he walked, he became aware of how good it felt to be outside, even with the drizzle. How idiotic last night had been. Not only in outcome, but it cost him most of today—a Sunday in San Francisco and the chance to roam from early morning until nightfall.

Daniel had never lived in San Francisco, but it had always been his favorite city. He still remembered his first visit, at age eleven, when he and his older brother walked all over, going up and down the monumental hills. They discovered some great vantage points, particularly of the bridges and bay. On later visits, he would explore the city's architecture and numerous ethnic districts. More recently, it had been enough to inhale the fresh air and imagine himself residing here.

After reaching Union Square, perhaps lured by childhood recollections, he decided to tackle Nob Hill. His goal, far up, almost a mile away, was California Street, with its array of famous hotels. As he labored up Powell Street, a passing cable car clanged a greeting, and several passengers waved. He smiled back. The memory of last night hadn't faded, but this was a new day.

He'd always felt lucky in San Francisco. As if anything were possible. There was freedom of thought here and the assimilation of countless lifestyles. Intellect was welcome, yet so was the absurd or outrageous.

About nine o'clock the previous night, driving his Buick across the Bay Bridge after his journey from L.A., he'd felt the same intense rush he'd experienced with his first glimpse of the city nearly forty years before. The lights, multitudinously-shaped buildings, and shimmering water beneath the span had lost none of their magic. Even with his recent losses so fresh in mind, he was optimistic. He'd chosen the right place to start a new life.

His climb up Nob Hill reminded him that he was no longer eleven. He stopped to catch his breath at a little park off California Street, which presented a splendid view of the nearby renowned Grace Cathedral. He counted half a dozen historic hotels in the vicinity. The drizzle had stopped, and he spotted two small girls on swings about fifty yards away, a man and a woman standing beside them. Undoubtedly it was his mood, but he saw a resemblance to his own two daughters a few years earlier.

Sunday was the day he and his wife regularly took the girls out. Beaches, museums, gardens, zoos, concerts—the best of L.A. He usually made the arrangements, while his wife, a high school teacher, provided commentary. Afterward, they'd pick a restaurant they'd never tried before, for Sunday dinner.

His own current choice for Sunday dinner, his first meal of the day, was a little diner on his way back down the hill. He might have held out for fancier, except the drizzle started again, and he almost slipped on the sidewalk. It was dark by the time he finished and returned to his room, now clean.

A shower was his next order of business. The warm water soothed his arms and wrists. After drying off, he again looked at his face in the mirror, more closely than before. Still, no indication that he had been slapped. He examined his stomach, where she had punched him. There were no bruises, and it no longer hurt.

"Guess I was lucky."

He heard himself repeat the words he'd spoken that morning to the burly hotel guy. Though he didn't recognize it at the time, he'd been right. Things could have been much worse.

A car alarm went off in the parking lot, and he stepped to the window for a look outside. There was no clue as to which was the offending car, nor was anyone around. He noticed that the drizzle had stopped again. Silently he predicted that tomorrow would be nice and sunny.

⋅⟨❀⟩⋅

Daniel accomplished a lot the next day, Monday, his first workday in San Francisco. He stopped by the local branch office of the sports tour company with which he'd had very successful employment in L. A. for the prior 25 years and got acquainted with the personnel. From there, he went to a San Francisco outlet of his L.A. bank to withdraw funds and to make sure he had a ready source of cash. Next, he searched for a place to live.

What he found not far from Union Square was an old Victorian-style apartment-hotel, where he could reside either on a temporary or on a more permanent basis, his choice. He promptly rented a studio apartment, which was totally furnished, including a Murphy bed, which folded down right out of the wall. The place was fully accessorized, complete with kitchenware, bedding, and phone. Moving in required little more than a toothbrush and the clothes on his back.

When he got into bed at his new address at the end of the day, which did turn out sunny and nice as he'd silently predicted, he smiled to himself. He was now officially a resident of San Francisco.

꿏

Daniel sat by himself the next evening, Tuesday, at a corner table in a large old coffeehouse. It was in the Mission District, an area just southwest of downtown that he remembered from previous visits. Since getting there about an hour earlier, he'd nibbled at a slice of carrot cake and peeked intermittently at a mystery novel set in San Francisco, bought at a nearby bookstore.

Growing restless, he got up to examine a painting on the wall behind him. He recognized its expressionistic style, although he wasn't able to identify the artist. When the loud churning of an espresso machine interceded, he glanced toward it.

He gazed around the large room. About fifty people were there, representing a wide range of age and ethnicity. He couldn't avoid observing that this seemed an authentic microcosm of San Francisco, long acknowledged as a truly cosmopolitan city.

He experienced the urge to make contact. Converse with someone, anyone. And yet, as he looked around the room, he felt shy, distant, even alienated. Why couldn't he simply approach someone and begin an exchange? Had he become so disconnected that that wasn't possible? Shrugging, he quickly picked up his book and headed for the exit.

Outside, he was surprised by how warm it was, with the absence of any breeze. Unfortunately, the air smelled rancid, and the sidewalk was crowded. He heard music coming from a club, and he slipped inside and found a three-piece band performing. But there was nowhere to sit, nor could he place the type of music. Again, he felt uncomfortable, so he quickly returned outside and headed for his Buick, parked nearby. The air seemed no less rancid.

Driving off, he noticed a woman sitting on a bus bench. As he passed, he gazed at her in the dark, and she looked appealing. While he circled the block, her image remained—tall, shapely, blonde. At a red light that stubbornly refused to change, he gunned his engine impatiently. Nearing the bus bench again, he clucked his tongue when she was still there.

She nodded to him as he passed her once more. He slowed the car, then stopped it in the middle of the street. A horn honking angrily from behind informed him that he had halted traffic. He would have gone on, except he spotted her approaching image in his sideview mirror. She quickly opened his passenger door and slid into the front seat.

He immediately recognized his mistake. She might have been appealing once, but certainly no longer. Her blonde hair was dirty and stringy. Deep welts, not visible in the dark when he passed, disfigured her cheeks. And her clothes smelled even more rancid than the air.

"I'm sorry," he apologized.

"For what?" she questioned.

"For stopping."

"Oh," she murmured.

She shrunk down into the seat. Horns continued blaring around them, and he was eager to get going. He considered driving up the street with her in the car to ease traffic. But no, he quickly reached into a pocket, pulled out a twenty, and gave it to her.

"What's this for?" she asked.

"For my mistake," he replied, nudging her toward the door.

She opened the door, then hesitated. Horns kept honking. She turned toward him and smiled. For the first time, he could see that she had several teeth missing.

"If you change your mind, I'll be here," she grinned widely, displaying even more missing teeth while holding up the twenty. "You got credit toward anything you want."

She finally got out, and he rapidly drove off, almost before she closed the door. Several car horns gave him one last angry blast. Her odor permeated the car, and he made sure all his windows were wide open.

In the distance, he could make out the buildings of downtown, inciting him toward thought. Was what he had just done—seek contact with a strange woman, as he'd done so many times in L.A.—merely his attempt to counteract alienation? The alienation he felt in the coffeehouse earlier, and then at the club while the band played.

He further pondered what he'd just done. And began to chastise himself for it. After all, this wasn't the reason he'd come to San Francisco. No, wasn't he here because the city was supposed to inspire him and offer the opportunity to start a new life?

❦

"Hey, batter batter. Hey, batter batter."

While walking on a path in a park not far from San Francisco's Fisherman's Wharf the following Saturday afternoon, Daniel could hear redundant chatter coming from beyond a grove of trees. He moved past the trees and came upon a baseball field where about a dozen boys were practicing. They appeared to be pre-teen and, like at the coffeehouse he'd visited, represented various ethnic denominations. A short, muscular black man of about forty, likely their coach, stood near first base, hitting fungoes left-handed. As Daniel approached him, he observed that virtually the man's entire right arm was missing. Although hesitant, Daniel decided to force himself to speak.

"Need a hand?" he managed.

The man stopped hitting and looked at Daniel strangely, causing him to recognize his thoughtless choice of words. He wished he could disappear, or at least take them back. But the guy's response, made as he batted another ball, seemed to ignore any insult.

"Ever pitch batting practice?"

"Yeah," Daniel replied quickly. "Used to pitch in high school . . . about a hundred years ago."

"Get warmed up."

"Stanton," Daniel introduced himself.

"Coach Lawson . . . Robert Lawson," the man reciprocated, extending his single hand, which Daniel gladly shook.

Lawson instructed a smallish Asian kid to warm Daniel up, pointing them both to a spot down the right-field foul line. The kid tossed Daniel a baseball glove plus a ball, and they headed off. No question when leaving his new apartment, Daniel never expected to encounter a youth baseball team for which he'd be requested to pitch batting practice. Luckily he was wearing a red San Francisco 49ers cap and sweatshirt acquired at work; otherwise, he'd have felt even more out of place than he already did.

He flexed his right arm when he and the kid got to a bullpen mound in foul territory near a fence bordering the field. The youngster stood about forty feet away. Daniel tossed his first pitch. It landed some ten feet in front of the kid. He flexed his right arm again and tried another pitch. This one was only slightly better, landing a little closer to the boy. Finally, about ten tosses later, he managed to reach the kid.

"Ready out there?" Lawson shouted to them.

"As I'll ever be," Daniel muttered pretty much to himself.

"Hey, batter batter, hey, batter batter," the redundant chatter began again once Daniel got to the pitcher's mound in the center of the field.

A bulky Middle-Eastern kid stepped into the right-hand batter's box. He took a couple of practice swings. Once more, Daniel flexed his arm. He fired his first pitch. Consistent with most of them in the bullpen, it landed several feet short of his target—home plate. He tried another. Same result. He glanced at Lawson, who, standing in the same area near first base, his single hand on his left hip, looked disgruntled.

How stupid of him, Daniel, to think he could do this. Just because he'd pitched in high school decades before. He tried six or seven more pitches. None of them came close to where the bulky kid might hit them. In fact, Daniel seemed to be getting wilder with each succeeding toss. Mercifully, Lawson called an end to the embarrassment by summoning the boys into the first base dugout.

"Practice is same time next Saturday," he announced sternly. "Anyone late need not come."

He dismissed the boys with a simple flick of his wrist. A couple remained behind to gather equipment and put it into a large bag. Still embarrassed, Daniel's first inclination was to leave also. Something made him stay, however, and he cautiously approached Lawson.

"Warned you," he nervously laughed. "Been almost a hundred years."

The coach frowned. Daniel couldn't refrain from glancing at what was a boney stub of a right arm protruding only slightly from a T-shirted shoulder, and thinking how this handicap must surely inhibit his coaching ability. Especially since there was no sign of his having any help. Maybe these circumstances offered possibility.

"You practice every Saturday?" Daniel proceeded.

"'Less it rains."

"Bad as I was," Daniel ventured carefully, "don't think you'd give me another chance."

"There's only me," Lawson confirmed Daniel's supposition.

"That mean it's okay?"

"There's only me," Lawson repeated almost disinterestedly. "But in the meantime, I were you, I'd get in shape."

"I promise," Daniel enthused.

"One thing you should know about these kids," Lawson used a confiding tone. "Every one of them comes from a broken home."

"Looks like I'd fit right in," Daniel grumbled almost under his breath.

⚜

About eight hours later, during his second Saturday night in San Francisco, Daniel neared the rundown hotel he ended up in a week before. It was a nice evening for a walk, warm with only a slight breeze, and he didn't mind having to park several blocks away. Even though he took a different route, he did mind that the same decay and blight were evident. Earlier, while eating spaghetti dinner at an Italian restaurant in San Francisco's North Beach—a district known for writers and poets like Jack Kerouac and Allen Ginsberg, and as the birthplace of the Beat Generation in the 1950s and 60s—he remembered his offer to reward the burly hotel guy who'd rescued him.

He pressed the buzzer beside the hotel entrance. Like the prior week, it took a second attempt to get a response. When he finally was buzzed into the dismal lobby, he found the same thin dark man of the previous week on duty, sitting in the caged enclosure, eyes fixed on the old black-and-white television. He didn't even look up as Daniel approached, nor did he speak.

"That other guy," Daniel interceded. "The heavy one. Is he here?"

Still not glancing up, the thin man merely shook his head. Based on the dialogue coming from the TV. Daniel was able to determine that the program was a detective show. He vaguely recalled that the same show was on the prior week when he arrived with the woman in black. Again he noticed part of the seven in 1987 was missing in the calendar behind the guy.

"Be here later?" Daniel persisted.

Again the man shook his head. Daniel considered seeking more information, like when the burly guy would be on. He also pondered leaving reward money with this guy to forward. When the man's gaze never left the TV, Daniel recognized the futility of both. Shrugging, he headed for the door.

Back outside, he decided to walk some more. He didn't feel like going home. Not on a Saturday night, when he was alone. Through twenty-two years of marriage, he was rarely alone on Saturday night. Sunday, he and his wife took their daughters out, while Saturday, they went out together. Dinners, movies, plays, concerts, parties—all the normal things a man did with his wife.

As he walked, he noticed that the territory was becoming very familiar. By coincidence, or maybe not by coincidence, he passed the spot in front of the other hotel, where he first encountered the woman in black. He could almost feel her presence, standing there, coolly puffing on her cigarette, uttering instructions. He even looked up and down the street but saw no sign of her.

Walking on, he saw drug dealers and panhandlers, like the prior week. At a street corner, he passed a cluster of young women in skimpy, revealing outfits. Maybe he should head home. Or at least find a neighborhood with less temptation. Not that he was so familiar with other neighborhoods in San Francisco. Not like he was in L.A.

His thoughts turned to L.A. How if he wanted a woman there, he could find one within minutes, high-priced or otherwise. He knew exactly where to go for whatever category he desired. No doubt, if he were to develop a similar network in San Francisco, he'd have to work at it. But then that wasn't what he was supposed to be doing here, was it?

"Good-looking man like you shouldn't be alone on a Saturday night."

Were his ruminations that transparent? Could just anyone see how he felt about Saturday night? The words came from behind him, and he turned to see a young woman in an exquisite long blue evening dress. She had dusky blonde hair and a pretty face with a smallish, perfectly formed nose. He would have liked to appraise her figure, but the dress cloaked it.

"I have a room around the corner," she enticed. "In a hotel."

The mere mention of another hotel room in this neighborhood should have sent him dashing to his car. She walked up to him, however, smiling. Unlike the teeth of the unkempt woman who had gotten into his car a few days earlier, hers were flawless, none of them missing. The right side of her dress was strapless, offering a view of a bare shoulder. He decided to counter her proposal.

"Rather, go to my place."

"Then it's no place, honey. Not on our first date."

She abruptly pivoted and strutted away from him. He still couldn't evaluate her figure, obscured by the blue dress and dim street light. He could imagine it, though. Ample breasts and long sleek legs. A wave passed through him. He paused, aware that he was about to succumb to what he knew he shouldn't be doing in San Francisco. Then he began to follow her. When she stopped for a red light, he caught up.

"Change your mind?" she smiled.

"This hotel . . . ? Got any amenities?"

"Sure," she chuckled. "Even got some things the fancy hotels don't have."

The light changed, and he followed her across the street. He noticed that she wore blue spiked heels, exactly matching the color of her dress. They clicked against the pavement as she walked.

"You do have money, honey?" she queried.

"I do."

"Couple hundred. Minimum."

He nodded. It crossed his mind that she could be police. Something about the way she carried herself, though, told him that she wasn't.

They turned a corner, and he became aware of the smell of piss. Up ahead, about a dozen persons stood in front of a tattered hotel awning. As she approached them, they parted for her, clearing a path, and he followed. He detected another sickening smell—seemingly a mixture of B. O. and booze. She pulled open a rusted gated door and closed it firmly behind them. They entered a small lobby with torn carpet and paint chipping off the walls.

"Impressive," he whistled.

"Nothing but the finest," she grinned, "for our first date."

They came upon a desk clerk at the end of the lobby. Daniel half-expected him to be thin and dark like the man at the other hotel, but this one was just the opposite—bulky and very pale. This week's rate was twenty dollars, instead of the ten he paid the previous Saturday. Did that mean the room would be twice as nice, or was he in for double the trouble? The clerk handed her a key, and they walked down a long corridor. She unlocked their door and guided him into the room. When she flicked on a light inside, he saw several roaches scurry along the bare floor.

"You keep good company," he quipped.

"In my profession, I meet nothing but the best," she winked.

He started to laugh but stopped himself. Instead, he diligently inspected the room, looking under the bed and into dresser drawers. Besides the entrance, there were two other doors. He opened them both and was surprised to find a closet and bathroom. So there was some logic to the price of these rooms, after all.

"No worries," she commented as he completed his survey. "No unwelcome intruders."

"What about the roaches?" he asked, pointing to a couple of others sprinting across the floor.

"They're not intruders," she winked again. "They live here."

"Obviously."

"Go ahead and take your clothes off," she said before disappearing into the bathroom.

He opted to wait. The room was cold, and he'd spent enough time in cold rooms lately, without clothes. Careful not to step on any roaches, he made his way to the bed and sat down. He heard the toilet in the bathroom flush, and the water faucet turned on and off. When she returned, she frowned at his inertia.

"I need some inspiration," he explained.

"Like what?"

"Like you taking off some of *your* clothes."

"Not without money, honey."

"Make you a deal," he offered while getting up and removing his wallet from a pants pocket.

"Yeah?"

"You take something off, I'll take something off," he suggested, dropping a couple of fifties on the bed. "You take something off. I'll take something off. Tit for tat."

"You be tat," she grinned. "And I'll be tit."

"Suits me just fine."

Still grinning, she unzipped her dress and slowly slid it down, then stepped out of it. She still had on only blue—brassiere, panties, stockings, heels—and her figure was even better than he'd anticipated. Her legs *were* long and sleek, and her breasts full. Plus, well-developed muscles made clear that she spent plenty of time in a gym.

He took off his jacket and put it on a chair. She kicked off her heels. Next came his shirt. When she unclasped her brassiere and flipped it onto the bed, he whistled inwardly at the beauty of her breasts. He liked this game of "tit for tat."

Eyeing the floor for darting roaches, he slipped off his shoes. She smiled at him, then slowly, teasingly, slid down her panties. Another wave passed through him, and he noticed that his hands were shaking as he took off his pants.

"Sorry," she said.

"For what?"

"For keeping my stockings on."

"Oh?"

"My one sacred rule. I never take everything off."

He didn't mind. Her blue nylons only heightened his desire. She went to the bed, scooped up the two fifties, and tucked them into her left stocking. Next, she took a condom package from inside her right stocking, unwrapped it, gestured him over to her, pulled down his boxers, and skillfully positioned the condom. He could feel her warm breath on his face.

"You will pay the other hundred?" she half-asked, half-commanded, holding his condomed dick. "Upon satisfaction."

"You're incredible," he said, shaking his head. "Beautiful. Talented. And a math whiz too."

"Got to be good with money, honey. In this business."

Without further dialogue, she kneeled and took his dick into her mouth, her ample breasts grazing his legs. He gasped in pleasure. Then she led him to the bed, laid down on it, and summoned him on top of her. When she guided his dick inside her, he gasped again. Using fingers on both hands, she made sure the condom stayed in place. His climax was quick and strong.

"Been a while," she teased.

"How could you tell?" He forced an embarrassed grin.

Without answering, she agilely slid out from under him. She rapidly gathered her clothes and returned to the bathroom. Once more, he heard the toilet flush and faucet turned on and off. Carefully watching where he was stepping, he went over to the chair where he'd put his clothes. He dressed slowly. Another roach dashed across the floor. He noticed the squashed remains of a second one on the wall above the bed. Remembering that he owed her more money, he dropped a hundred dollar bill on the bed. Then he sat down on the bed, keeping his feet elevated off the floor. Finally, she came out of the bathroom, looking just as comely in her blue dress as when she first approached him on the street.

"Maybe we can go to your place next time," she offered, taking the money off the bed.

"Good," he replied, nodding toward another roach racing across the floor. "We can be alone."

She chuckled. Then she went to the door and opened it. When he lingered on the bed, she looked at him impatiently.

"What're you waiting for?" she asked, a little snarl in her voice.

"For you to tell me what this hotel has that the fancy ones don't," he answered, finally getting up. "Like you said on the street."

"You just stepped on one," she smirked, pointing to another squashed roach mere inches from his shoe.

He laughed and followed her out the door. As they walked down the long corridor, he wondered if the roaches were there too, or if they confined their habitation to the rooms. Or, very unlikely, he realized, to only the room he and she had just vacated.

Outside the hotel, the crowd on the sidewalk again parted for her. He followed her along the sidewalk, tracing their original path in reverse. Reaching the place where they first met, she stopped. When he passed her on the way to his car, she completely ignored him. No tearful good-byes. Nor even the slightest hint that they had just spent intimate time together.

While walking on, he noticed that the air seemed cooler, and the piss smell less evident. He also noticed a young woman standing against a tall apartment building. Although it was difficult to see in the dim, shadowy street light, and her long dark hair partially concealed her face, he could tell she was pretty. She was simply dressed—jeans and a pullover top—and looked to be very thin.

"Hello," he smiled.

She ignored him. In fact, she glanced the other way. He went a few steps past her, then doubled back. This time he nodded at her as he went by. Once more, she gazed away.

He turned around again and, still getting no favorable response from her, walked on. The woman in black entered his thoughts one more time. He imagined her standing over him as she had last week. She wore only a black brassiere and panties. He felt the familiar stirring. Maybe he should go back to the spot where they'd met. But it was late, past midnight, now Sunday morning.

Saturday night had ended.

Chapter Three

Standing on the pitcher's mound in the center of the same baseball field he'd discovered the previous Saturday, Daniel was sweating profusely. He'd already thrown some 25 pitches of batting practice and was very tired. Even the youngsters behind him calling out their repetitive "Hey, batter batter, hey, batter batter," failed to energize him. He wasn't going to quit, though. Not with Robert Lawson—stationed near first base, lone hand on hip, expression stern—watching him so intently.

Daniel tossed his next pitch. Alfredo Campas, a husky right-handed batter with a large head and dark wavy hair, swung hard and connected. The ball flew far down the left-field line, hooking foul by several feet. Daniel took a deep breath and peeked at Lawson, hopefully.

"Okay," the coach yelled out, maybe receiving Daniel's silent message, "everyone over here."

Relieved, Daniel breathed deeply again. Likely his pitching stint for the afternoon was over. Despite his following Lawson's advice about conditioning—by going to the park every day after work, playing catch there, and jogging—it hadn't done much good.

"We practice next Saturday," Lawson instructed after all the kids and Daniel joined him near first base. "Same time. Remember, anyone late need not come."

Because no one had been tardy for the start of practice a couple of hours earlier, all twelve players for the Orioles—Daniel's new team—were present. Lawson had welcomed him with a green cap with Orioles insignia on it, a little orange bird. As the new assistant coach, before pitching batting practice, he'd already offered bunting tips, shown how to tag baserunners sliding into bases, and taught pitchers the circular way to cover first base on balls hit to the right side of the infield.

With a flip of his lone hand, Lawson dismissed the youngsters. Like the prior week, a couple stayed behind to pick up equipment. After they'd finished, one of them—Alfredo Campas, the final hitter—approached Lawson.

"Coach, you help me hit better?"

"Ask Coach Stanton, Alfredo."

"Coach, you help me hit better?" Alfredo inquired after turning to Daniel. "I hit too many foul ball."

Daniel acknowledged Alfredo's admission by patting the boy on the back and taking a bat from the equipment bag. He led him to home plate. A slight breeze had kicked up, and he appreciated its cooling effect, especially since he was still perspiring.

While pitching him batting practice, Daniel had observed Alfredo's tendency to step *away* from pitches with his front leg, the left, rather than into them. The usual result, like on Daniel's final pitch, was a foul ball outside third. Daniel had in mind helping Alfredo adjust his swing according to the location of the pitch.

"If the ball's over the outside part of the plate, hit it to right field," he explained while standing in the batter's box and stepping *into* an imaginary pitch while swinging. "If it's inside, then it's okay to pull it to left."

"I understand, Coach. I will practice every night at my house."

"Try it now."

Daniel handed him the bat. Alfredo exhibited quick learning by stepping into an imaginary outside pitch and pretending to hit it to right field. Next, he stepped away from an imaginary inside pitch and pretended to pull it to left.

"Good, Alfredo."

"I will practice every night at my house, Coach."

Daniel patted him on the back again. The boy picked up his glove and headed off. Daniel took the bat over to where Lawson was standing and put it back into the equipment bag.

"You can see his home from here," Lawson said, pointing toward a large house across the street from the field.

"That two-story gray?" Daniel asked while pointing toward it also.

"Right. It's a foster home. Six kids live there. Alfredo was orphaned as a baby. Never knew his parents."

"He has a sad look," Daniel expressed as he watched Alfredo in the distance, walking toward the house.

"Nothing a few base hits wouldn't cure," Lawson asserted.

⁂

Another Saturday night. Another trip to the rundown hotel he'd visited the prior two Saturday nights. Ostensibly to deliver the reward money he'd promised the burly guy who'd rescued him after that first night. Even he, Daniel, wasn't convinced that that was his entire motive.

This time none of the characters from the hotel were there. A different man was at the desk—rugged-looking, with heavily-tattooed arms—watching the black-and-white TV. Apparently, he didn't speak English because when Daniel addressed him, he shook his finger, "no." Evidently, Daniel wouldn't locate the burly guy tonight, nor did he decide to leave the money behind for him with this man.

He departed the hotel. It was still early, and he wasn't thrilled with the idea of returning to his apartment. Besides, it was Saturday night. He decided to roam.

Ground fog made the air seem thick. He passed the hotel in front of which he first met the woman in black; however, she wasn't there. Like the previous week, he checked up and down the street. No sign of her. A guy with a portable radio held to his ear yelled something incomprehensible at him. Daniel ignored him. He couldn't ignore the smell of piss though, which, probably because of the fog, seemed more pungent than the week before.

Walking on, he spotted the hotel he'd gone to with the woman in the blue evening dress. The crowd gathered in front looked no different than then, and he doggedly fought his way through them. No one stepped aside for him, as they had for her. Like then, he couldn't avoid the sickening smell of B.O. and booze.

He kept going. Several young women wearing scanty outfits stood on the sidewalk near a street corner. He wondered if the women ever got cold. One of them gestured to him, but he continued. For some reason, the piss smell diminished.

Up ahead, he noticed the same young woman he'd seen the prior week, standing in dim light against the same tall apartment building. She wore a similar casual outfit—jeans and a pullover top, both light-colored. A small black backpack lay on the sidewalk beside her. Again her long dark hair partially covered her face.

"Hello," he greeted, passing her.

She ignored him, like before.

Like before, she looked pretty. He moved closer to where he could almost touch her. She simply turned away.

"I don't mean to bother you."

His words appeared to echo off the apartment building wall. She didn't reply. He knew he should leave, except something about her held him. Probably the way she seemed to be seeking invisibility. Much different than the woman in black, who was so direct and conspicuous, especially for this neighborhood.

"I guess you don't like me."

Once more, his words bounced off the wall. Once more, she ignored him. No question, he should go. He pivoted to walk away.

"I don't know you," she said softly.

"My name's Daniel," he replied right away, turning back toward her. Surprised that she had spoken, he virtually blurted out the words almost incoherently. Of course, he was eager to continue the dialogue. Too bad that didn't occur right away.

"Do you live around here?" he tried after another uncomfortable silence.

Again no reply. Once more, he considered leaving. Wasn't he merely embarrassing them both? Why not just be satisfied that he'd eked out a few words from her? Shrugging glumly, he retreated a couple of steps. Again she surprised him by speaking.

"I'm not like the other girls around here."

"I can see that," he managed, moving toward her once more.

"Then what do you want from me?"

"Maybe . . . a little conversation," he answered carefully.

"That's all?"

His only response was a slight head bob. Really, at that moment, he wasn't certain what he wanted from her. And no question, he realized that he might be headed for trouble.

"Do you have money for a room?" she continued.

"Yes."

"I know a nice place . . . Out of this neighborhood."

He smiled at her words, although he wasn't sure which appealed to him more—"nice place" or "out of this neighborhood." He picked up her backpack and handed it to her. As she put her hands and arms through the straps and they began walking, he refrained from asking her what was inside of it. She walked on his inside, nearer the buildings. He noticed that the route she picked seemed dark and desolate, with few people in sight. He considered suggesting his apartment, then realized that was a bad idea. He'd gotten this far with her—why take a chance on retarding further progress?

"My name is Christina."

"Christina," he replied. "That's nice."

Other than her giving directions, those words were their only conversation until they reached their destination, a hotel with a red awning that extended along the sidewalk to the street. She did stop before they arrived to pet a dog after nodding to its owner. While she was doing that, he reminded himself that when they were finished, he'd have to double back to get his car, which they'd coincidentally passed along the way.

At this hotel, he paid forty dollars—double the rate of the prior one. And he was required to register. Also, this hotel had an elevator to take them up to the fourth floor. Going down the hallway, he observed that the carpeting wasn't frayed. And there was an ice machine, a luxury he hadn't seen in either previous hotel. Inside the room, once she turned on an overhead light, he was surprised by a TV with remote, plus a coffee maker. And yes, even a phone. All of which provided further evidence that there was some sense to the cost of these various hotel rooms.

She went to a window and opened it slightly. She inspected the carpet, bedding, and two chairs in the room. He considered asking her what she was looking for. But before the words came out, still toting her backpack, she headed for the bathroom.

Once she disappeared, he switched on two bright table lamps. He anticipated the illumination inciting a bevy of roaches to scurry across the floor, but none were visible. Her inspection reminded him to conduct one of his own—of the closet and dresser drawers. He found nothing unusual. She came out of the bathroom; her long dark hair tied neatly behind her with a yellow ribbon.

"Very pretty," he praised, sitting down on one of the chairs.

"My hair?" she frowned. "You don't know how much work it takes."

"Looks like it's worth it to me."

Disregarding his comment, she chain-locked the door and stepped back to the window she'd opened. She drew back its curtain slightly for a glimpse outside. Then she sat down on the nearby bed and removed a small brown pipe from her backpack. She also took out a tiny tin can and sprinkled some of its ingredients into the pipe. Although he wasn't sure exactly what she was doing, he could see that she was using a hairpin as a sort of blender. No doubt someone else would have been bored watching her, but he wasn't. It occurred to him that she was probably less than half his age.

Apparently satisfied with her preparations, she placed the pipe on a nightstand. She got up and centered a picture that was above the bed. She adjusted a lampshade that was slightly askew. The curtains covering the open window, allowing too much illumination from a street light outside, needed closing. Next, she turned on the TV and channel-surfed until she ran across an old Humphrey Bogart movie.

"Oh, good," she congratulated herself. "Lauren Bacall."

She sat back down on the bed and lit the pipe with a lighter extracted from her backpack. A pillow she fluffed became her backrest. The tension and unapproachability he'd observed when he'd first spoken to her appeared to have been completely replaced by a state of utter relaxation. A state which her first drag from the pipe rudely interrupted.

"This shit's awful," she choked. She choked a second time, followed by several rasping coughs. "You're going to have to excuse me."

He didn't know what to say. She got up from the bed and moved quickly to the door. Evidently, as an afterthought, she returned to the bed for her backpack. Then she headed again for the door before stopping a couple of steps short of it.

"Oops," she laughed nervously. "Forgot . . . No money. Could you loan me a twenty?"

He remained silent. The only sounds in the room came from the movie on the TV, in which Humphrey Bogart and Lauren Bacall seemed in some kind of trouble. Finally, he shrugged, took a twenty from his wallet, and handed it to her.

"I'll be back soon," she promised. "Let me know what happens to Lauren Bacall."

She left the room before he could answer. He stepped over to the window, hoping to see if she departed the hotel. The sidewalk in front wasn't visible, though. He glanced around the room and observed that she'd taken everything with her, including her pipe. He concluded that she wouldn't be back—twenty dollars plus some brief shelter had no doubt been all she wanted.

Even with the open window, he suddenly felt very warm. As if he might be getting sick. He realized there was no sense in staying. He wasn't interested in the movie, so why not get his car and head home? Besides, he hadn't come to San Francisco to be in a hotel room with a woman he didn't know, had he?

There was a knock at the door. It couldn't be her returning this quickly. And she couldn't have forgotten something because she'd taken everything with her, including his twenty. Unless she wanted more money from an easy mark like him. He went to the TV and turned down the volume.

"Who's there?" he called out.

"Sorry, pal," a male voice answered. "Wrong room."

He immediately recalled the guy who knocked at his door at the rundown hotel in the middle of the night while he lay handcuffed. "Sorry, man, wrong room, wrong floor." He paced the room. He was so vulnerable. What if the young woman had set him up to be robbed and beaten by some of her friends, as the woman in black had threatened to do? Maybe the guy who'd just knocked was simply checking to make sure he was still there.

He noticed that she'd also taken the room key. Anyone she gave it to could use it. He chain-locked the door as she had done and looked around for something he could use for a weapon. He saw nothing.

Another knock. He edged back to the door and put his ear to it. The only thing he could hear was street noise coming from the open window.

"Who is it?" he asked softly.

"Christina, silly. Who do you think?"

"You alone?"

"Of course."

He opened the door only as far as the chain allowed. She seemed to be alone. He unbolted the chain and opened the door wider. He peeked out into the hall and saw no one behind her.

"I'm the one supposed to be paranoid," she laughed, slipping into the room.

"Sorry."

"Well? What happened?"

"What do you mean?" he asked, clueless.

"Lauren Bacall," she replied, moving to the TV.

"Oh . . . Sorry."

She waved forgiveness. Still watching the movie, she went to the bed and began to mix a new blend for her pipe. He admired her diligence and her ability to follow the movie at the same time. Again, Humphrey

Bogart and Lauren Bacall were in jeopardy; however, he kept his focus on Christina. Taking the first drag from her pipe, she leaned back against a pillow.

"Crack cocaine?" he guessed.

"Yeah," she reported. "Much better shit this time."

He didn't respond. Although he'd done no more than occasionally dabble in drugs over the years, he understood that they were a significant part of this scene. At times he caught himself mentally criticizing others when they used, but he always tried to keep his thoughts to himself. After all, what others did was none of his business. Plus, he, of all people, had no right to judge nor make any attempt to uphold the law or any specific moral code.

As he sat down in the same chair, she took another drag. Once more, he noticed the relaxed state she'd achieved. It made him aware that she seemed a study in contradiction. Her current tranquility and her earlier remoteness were mere masks for the vitality and energy bubbling inside her. For evidence, all he had to do was recall her buzzing around the room, mixing her pipe, acquiring new drugs, and keeping tabs on the movie.

"It's warm in here," she said, fanning herself with one hand.

She got up and took off her blue top. As if he wasn't there. She was very thin, her ribs jutting out below a frilly white brassiere. He wondered whether her legs were also slim.

"Make yourself comfortable," he asserted sarcastically.

"You're not Jack the Ripper?"

"Depends on who you talk to," he admitted. "Me and Jack, we both had our problems with the law."

"That makes three of us," she smiled.

She was still watching the movie. He got up from his chair and stepped slowly over to the bed. Tentatively, while her eyes were still on the TV, he kissed her lightly on the forehead.

"What's that for?" she asked, looking surprised.

"For good luck."

In truth, he wasn't sure what it was for. Clearly, he liked her, but he wasn't clear in what way. A father separated from his own two daughters, seeking a substitute? Certainly, she was young enough to be his daughter. Or was it something more straightforward? Like simple sexual desire. Another possibility—was he experiencing initial romantic stirrings for a young woman he considered attractive?

"Where do you live?" he questioned, sitting back down in the chair.

"Does it matter?"

"No. Just curious."

"You think I'm a fucking bag lady," she accused.

"No. I don't."

"Well, you're right. I'm not."

The tone of her last words inferred finality, and he was wise enough not to pursue the subject. She kept on smoking her pipe and watching the movie, contraction of facial muscles suggesting heightened interest in the latter whenever Lauren Bacall encountered distress. He continued being far more attentive to Christina than to the TV. At times she had a faraway gaze as if she'd entered a meditative state. He wondered who she was and what in her background had brought her to this place in life. He concluded that there were plenty of things about her that he'd be better off not knowing.

When the film ended, she went into the bathroom again. He weighed his prospects. Should he propose sex? It had already been determined that she wouldn't refuse money, and he surmised that she'd accept any reasonable offer. Didn't she make her willingness clear by readily taking off her top? Yet something told him to be patient, that it would be better to take his time with her, that there might be more at stake here than easy intimacy. Despite his wanting to stay, the idea of leaving was gaining momentum.

"Time for me to go," he quickly greeted her exit from the bathroom. She was still topless except for her brassiere.

"What do you mean?" she challenged. "We haven't even . . ."

"You asked me what I wanted from you. I *told* you . . . maybe a little conversation."

"And no fucking more?" she amped up resistance, her expression one of surprise. "But that . . ."

"I like you," he blurted, interrupting. "And I'd like to see you again."

"You know where to find me."

"You won't ignore me next time?"

"I don't ignore people I know," she said while sitting down on the bed again. She took another drag from her pipe.

"I might have given up."

"You might've been Jack the Ripper."

"I might still be him," he smiled. "Reincarnated."

"Reincarnated?" she questioned enthusiastically. "You believe in that?"

"Believe in what?" he puzzled.

"Reincarnation, silly."

Having little knowledge of the subject, he shook his head. She took another drag. Neither of them spoke for several seconds.

"I believe in it," she broke the silence.

"Oh."

"Anyway, I have to be careful about who I take here. Plus . . . I'm fucking shy at first."

"You'd never know it," he laughed, eyeing her top, lying on the bed.

She laughed too, before taking one more drag. She used the remote to channel surf again. After muttering something which he construed as displeasure at what was on, she turned off the TV. He got up from the chair and started toward the door.

"Oh, forgot to mention," she smiled impishly, a twinkle in her eye. "There's a penalty for leaving early."

"A penalty?"

"Yes."

"What?"

"Another twenty."

He didn't hesitate about giving her money this time. In fact, he took two twenties from his wallet and handed them both to her. She promptly tried to give one back. He shook his head in refusal.

"Okay," she relented. "I'll keep it . . . On one condition."

"What?"

"It's not a gift. It's a loan."

"Sure," he nodded, sarcasm in his voice. "It's a loan."

"Let's shake on it," she insisted.

She took his hand, and, without much enthusiasm, he allowed her to shake it. He kissed her forehead again, touching her arm in the process. He immediately became aware of how thin it felt. He wondered if she'd soon be back on the street that night. He was afraid he knew the answer.

After shutting the door behind him out in the hallway, he thought about what to do next. It wasn't too late to find another woman. But he knew he wouldn't even try. He knew he'd go right to his car and drive straight back to his apartment.

Chapter Four

"Ever hear of the Big Brothers?" Robert Lawson asked Daniel.

"You mean that program for boys from broken homes? And guys who sponsor them?"

"Yep. I been a big brother more than fifteen years. Got three kids right now."

"Really," Daniel replied, beginning to have an idea where this was headed.

He and Lawson had just finished conducting another Saturday Orioles' team practice and were standing near home plate. Alfredo had just left, following another brief batting session with Daniel. The boy had shown that he was continuing to learn what Daniel was trying to teach him--by stepping into an imaginary pitch and hitting it to right field with his bat.

"You're doing a nice job with that kid," Lawson went on.

"Thanks."

"Ever think about joining?" Lawson questioned softly.

"The Big Brothers?"

"Sure."

"Don't think I'd qualify," Daniel admitted uncomfortably after a slight hesitation.

"I know the local director."

"But you don't know the problems I've had."

"With the law?"

"'Fraid so."

"Nothin' to do with kids?" Lawson asked, looking concerned.

"No, no. Nothing like that?"

Out in the field, a couple of boys began to toss a football. Daniel started to feel cold as a late-afternoon March breeze began to kick up. He pulled his jacket tight around him, then zipped it up. In fact, the day had been the coldest since his arrival in San Francisco, the temperature only reaching the mid-fifties. Lawson continued to look concerned.

"Don't mean to pry . . ." he said.

"Too much time on the streets." Daniel could hear the embarrassment in his voice.

"You don't look like a druggie."

"That's not it," Daniel muttered almost under his breath. "It's . . . ladies."

Lawson frowned. Daniel gazed off into the distance toward the two kids, who began to kick the football. When he resumed talking, he purposely avoided looking at Lawson.

"I'm trying to get away from that stuff. Here in San Francisco."

"San Francisco might not be the best place to get away from . . . ladies. How you doing so far?"

"So far, not so good. I met a girl, though. Maybe she'll help."

"Street girl?"

Daniel fidgeted with his Orioles cap.

"Watch yourself," Lawson advised. "Anyway, working with kids'll help. Take your mind off that other stuff."

"Alfredo," Daniel tried to build on Lawson's theme, "you said he was orphaned as a baby."

"Story is," Lawson seemed happy to recount, "his mother wanted to give him a better life. She sneaked into this country from Mexico. Died giving birth, but Alfredo was born here. Which makes him a citizen."

"What about his father?"

"No record of him."

"Some story."

"I can talk to my friend at the Big Brothers," Lawson offered.

Daniel gazed off at the two kids again. They had started tackling each other. Then he looked back to Lawson and nodded slightly.

⋰⊙⋱

Another Saturday night. Daniel drove by Christina's "spot," but she wasn't there. He passed a second time. No luck.

What to do next? He decided to try to improve on his initial less-than-stellar foray into the Mission District, when he encountered the blondish woman with the missing teeth and bad B. O. Later, he could double back and go by Christina's "spot" again.

This time, instead of a coffeehouse and club in the Mission, he tried a theater offering reprise films. The décor inside was austere—plain walls and dingy seats, some of which he discovered broken. The atmosphere accurately foreshadowed the movie, a French noir account of a civil servant who, after losing his job, turned to mass murder for revenge.

If the theater and film fell slightly short of entirely depressing Daniel, the environment outside completed the task. Things seemed even grimmer than on his other occasion here. Drug dealers and panhandlers solicited him. Angry faces were everywhere. And when he eventually returned to his car, he wasn't exactly cheered by the sight of a guy peeing next to it.

Driving off, he wondered where to next. He thought of Christina again. Maybe she'd be in her "spot" by now.

He noticed a woman walking on the sidewalk ahead. She had long dark hair like Christina's. And she had on an outfit like what Christina had worn—jeans and a casual top. Although appearing older and larger than Christina, she did look attractive.

He drove past, hoping for a closer look. The darkness stymied him. She waved to him, but he didn't trust stopping for her because of his previous experience in this area. Instead, he turned right, onto a side street, and using a driveway, quickly turned around and eased to a corner where he anticipated her passing directly in front of him.

His maneuver worked perfectly. She walked within five feet of his car. And yes, she did look attractive. Also, her smile, as she glanced at him, reminded him of Christina's. When he didn't look away, she motioned him to roll down his passenger window.

"Can I get in?"

She didn't wait for a reply. She simply opened the door and slid into the car. He assumed that she wasn't police because she'd have never gotten in. Still, he was wary, especially in this neighborhood. At least her aroma was pleasant as she edged over beside him—fresh like she'd just bathed. A small scar on her left cheek, barely visible in the dim light, compromised her appearance only slightly.

"Where to?" he inquired, peeking nervously at his rearview mirror.

"Parking lot," she informed.

"Which one?"

"You don't know?"

"No."

"You're not from around here . . ."

"No," he acknowledged.

"You got money?"

"Yes."

"I knew you're not a cop," she reported matter-of-factly.

"How?"

"This street . . . Local gangs, they shoot at cops here."

Her comment certainly didn't improve his mood. He thought about trying to get away from her and leave the area. But then he considered the possible risk. She, an angry woman in this neighborhood. Where he was an outsider.

She directed him to turn his car around, and he obliged. The parking lot was only a block away, next to a school. She pointed him to a dark corner. Another car was already in the lot, and he eyed it suspiciously. Before switching off his engine, he carefully shut all the windows and locked the doors.

"You worry too much," she accused.

"You just mentioned shootings."

"At cops. Not people."

"Oh," he feigned relief.

"You want me to unbutton my top?"

"Whatever you'd like."

"What I'd like is fifty bucks."

He took two twenties and a ten from his wallet and gave them to her. After unbuttoning her top, she put his left hand on her right breast. He stroked it a little, becoming aware of its rough texture. She unzipped her jeans and slid them down her thighs. She placed his right hand in her uncovered crotch. He wondered where she'd put the third hand if he had one. He had a pretty good idea.

"Now you," she commanded, reaching to unbuckle his belt.

He could only admire her skill. Within seconds, she had his pants down, a condom in place, his dick in her mouth. He couldn't help thinking that if this was a speed contest, she would easily win. And, still eyeing the other car, he was grateful for her efficiency.

"We'd be more comfortable in the back seat," she advised.

"No, this is fine."

He grew tense when the other car, headlights off, came toward them. It passed them, however, turned left, exited the lot, then headed off. He felt himself breathe deeply in relief. Or maybe it was because she was still at work on his dick—mouth and fingers encouraging him toward completion. Something which she achieved readily, even in this bleak environment.

"You're very talented," he praised, quickly zipping his pants and buckling his belt.

"So I've been told. And you didn't even get the best part."

"Didn't need to."

She probably didn't hear his last comment because she'd already opened the door, buttoning her top and zipping her jeans in the process. Without so much as a single parting word, she slammed the door and began crossing the parking lot. The instant she was out of sight, he started his car and drove toward the exit. At the street, he looked around for any possible trouble, then turned right—opposite the direction she'd headed—and sped off.

He thought of Christina again almost immediately. It still wasn't late, and he could get to her spot in ten minutes. But wait—shouldn't she be his first choice for any night, not his second or third?

He began to look for someone else. Like he'd done so often in L.A. the previous ten years or so. Finish one encounter, then seek another. And when he was done with that one, go for another. And maybe after that, still one more.

Once he'd gotten started, his quest could be virtually unending. His behavior was so predictable and repetitive that it was like he was in prison. All self-control would vanish. He suddenly understood that the essence of his life in L.A. the last ten years had really been not much more than a prison.

While he drove on, the buildings of downtown came into sight. As they had that other night he'd been in the Mission District. Prompting him to recall once more that San Francisco was supposed to inspire a new life. Clearly, he hadn't made much progress.

Again his thoughts turned to Christina. To how he saw her as zestful, free-spirited, and offbeat—pretty much the way he viewed San Francisco. Maybe she could propel him out of the rut he was in. Maybe she could inspire him toward making some real changes.

While he was stopped at a red light, his thoughts were interrupted by the outline of a woman walking on a sidewalk ahead. A seemingly attractive woman signaling him as he drove by once the light changed. He braked briefly after passing her. Then he gunned his accelerator and sped off toward his apartment.

⚜

Daniel was growing more and more concerned. He went by Christina's spot several times during the ensuing week, but she wasn't there. Had something happened to her? Or had she found a new place from which to operate? One that he had no way of knowing about.

It was another Saturday night. Things seemed different, though, because of wet streets and sidewalks and the presence of umbrellas and raincoats. As he walked toward her spot once more, after having parked a couple of blocks away, a sloshing car fishtailed nearby on the street. The rain, which had been steady all day—causing Lawson to cancel that afternoon's regular baseball practice—became heavier. Whipped by a howling wind, it slapped against the umbrella Daniel held up and began to get him wet.

Before leaving his apartment, he'd vowed that his sole purpose was to find Christina, without deviation. No rundown hotels. No side trips into blighted areas or conversations with strangers. He'd already encountered a woman on a street corner who addressed him, but he proceeded on.

Aside from whether Christina would be there and the issues involved if she wasn't, two other questions troubled him as he neared the apartment building wall. If she was there, would she even remember him? After all, their one short meeting had taken place a full two weeks earlier. And if she did remember him, would she be happy to see him?

He tried to brace himself for negative answers to these questions. He got within view of the wall, yet he had difficulty seeing in the rain. He moved closer and stuck out a hand to enhance visibility. Once again, for the sixth or seventh time that week, no Christina.

What to do now? Wait there with the windswept rain splattering against his umbrella and him, hoping she might come? She'd probably already found someone for the night and was tucked away in a hotel room, cozy and warm, while he stood there like an imbecile, getting drenched. Also, there were those other troubling possibilities. Shouldn't he simply get out of there, go home, and dry off?

He compromised. He noticed a little market up the street and ducked inside. He killed a little time by wandering down an aisle, searching for a snack. It did occur to him that he could pass the time by trying to find another woman as he'd done on the past three Saturday nights. But then he'd have to deal with the rain. Plus, he'd promised himself—no side trips. Instead, he picked out a candy bar and brought it to the cashier.

When he emerged from the market, the rain had diminished to not much more than a drizzle. He saw that someone was standing against the apartment building, maybe fifty feet away. Whoever it was held a blue umbrella in front of them, preventing identification. Moving closer, to within fifteen or twenty feet, he could see long dark hair. And yes, jeans and a casual top, beneath a green jacket. A gush of optimism passed through him. Waiting had paid off.

"Hi, Christina," he greeted cautiously, aware of his concerns regarding how she would relate to him at first.

"Hi," she smiled.

"You remember me."

"Of course." She continued smiling.

He liked the way she looked, brown eyes blinking up at him through the falling mist. She reached out and touched his hand, a gesture he considered very favorably. He dug into his jacket pocket and pulled out the candy bar.

"Want a bite?" He held it up.

"Sure."

He unwrapped the package and gave the bar to her. She took a little nibble, then a bigger bite. He laughed. When she returned the bar to him, he re-wrapped it and put it back into his pocket.

"Want to get a room?" he ventured, still cautious.

"Sorry. Can't right now."

"Oh."

"Meeting someone here in a few minutes."

"Oh," he repeated, disappointed, even though this type of rejection was on his earlier list.

"We could meet later," she offered brightly.

"When?"

"Maybe . . . couple hours. I could call you."

He weighed the prospect of returning in the rain. He was still disappointed that she wasn't available right then. Yet if she called, he knew he'd return.

"Daniel," she said, interrupting his thoughts.

"Yes," he replied more enthusiastically, surprised and pleased that she remembered his name.

"I'm happy you came. I was hoping you'd stop by like a couple weeks ago."

"And the week before that," he mumbled almost to himself.

"Do you want me to call you later?" she asked, ignoring his comment.

A nearby car honking, probably at her, deflected his attention briefly. Rather than answering her, he took a pen out and wrote his phone number on the back of a business card. The ink ran a little because of the rain, so he made sure she could read his number by having her recite it aloud. As she slipped the card into her backpack, he liked the way she smiled at him again.

"Daniel . . ."

"Yes?"

"You wouldn't have another twenty?"

He considered asking why she didn't get it from the person she was meeting. The rain picked up again, though, and so did the wind. Shrugging, he took out his wallet and gave her the money.

"It's not a gift," she stated definitively. "It's a loan."

"Sure. A loan."

He turned and headed up the street toward his car. He remembered the candy bar in his pocket and took it out. He started unwrapping it again, then changed his mind, deciding instead to wait until he got back to his place.

"Hey there, good-lookin'," someone called out to him. "Wanna go visit the roaches?"

He stopped walking. He saw the woman with the blue evening dress from three weeks before, standing next to a doorway. The image of all those scurrying roaches in the hotel room flooded his mind. Tonight her blonde hair was pulled to one side, revealing her left ear, and she had on a white miniskirt and orange sweater. The familiar wave passed through him. Then he remembered his vow. No deviation.

"No thanks," he answered.

"We could go to your place," she coaxed.

"No," he declared firmly. "No place."

He resumed walking. The rain seemed less severe.

❦

Daniel finally got into bed. He'd looked out his window about forty-five minutes earlier and found that the rain had stopped. Christina hadn't called after the couple of hours she'd spoken of. Nor had she called after three hours. Ditto for four.

Saturday night had become Sunday morning. He knew that falling asleep wouldn't be easy.

Chapter Five

"Tara, you know you're not supposed to talk to your father."

I imagined Mother's voice in my ears as I dialed Dad's number. Of course, I knew it was against her rules to phone him, but I just had to. After all, it had been nearly nine months since he left home, and I had to be sure he was all right.

I couldn't tell which sounded louder—the phone ringing on the other end of the line, or my heart thumping away in my chest. I'm pretty sure it was my heart. With each unanswered ring, my disappointment grew. He must have gone out. I didn't know whether I'd dare try him again.

"Hello."

I couldn't believe that he'd answered and I'd heard his voice. I could feel myself becoming flustered. It wasn't too late to hang up. I kept glancing at the painting of the ocean above my bed as if it would let me know what to do.

"Hi, Dad," I finally managed, my voice shaky.

"Tara . . . Is that you?"

"I almost gave up," I uttered feebly. "I didn't think you were going to answer the phone."

"Sorry. I've been out. I just got in from a walk. It's been raining here, and I wanted to get out before it started again."

"I know I'm not supposed to call," I spoke apologetically, pretty much duplicating Mother's imagined warning. "Your company . . . they gave me your number."

"Is everything okay?"

"Fine," I answered, looking at the painting of the ocean again. Even I could hear the doubt in my voice. I knew I should have hung up before, while I still had the chance.

"You sure everything's okay?" He seemed to grasp the level of my distress.

"Well . . . I miss you. Dad"

"I miss you too, Tara."

Neither of us spoke again right away. I could still hear my heart thumping. I could also hear the rain pattering against my window. His stormy weather must've reached here.

"Does your mother know we're talking?" he broke our silence.

"No, but I just had to be sure you're okay."

"How is your mother? And your sister?"

"Both fine."

"How's high school?"

"Not easy. I didn't think being a freshman would be this hard."

There was another pause. I took a deep breath. So many questions went through my mind. I still clearly recall the day Mother told Stacy and me that we couldn't see Dad again, or even talk to him. Mother didn't want to tell us why, but we insisted. We kept after her for weeks before she finally broke down and told us.

"Dad, I was wondering," I finally said.

"Yes, honey?"

"Why did you do what you did?" I asked carefully.

"Do what?"

"Mother told us what you did. Did we do something to let you down?"

"No, nothing," he answered quickly. "I was foolish, honey. I lost control."

"We didn't do something wrong? We couldn't have helped you?"

"No, Tara. It was all my fault. No one else had anything to do with it."

I didn't call to put him on the spot or to make him feel guilty, yet I knew from his tone that that's what I'd done. I wished I hadn't phoned.

And I wished I could take back those questions. Again I looked at the painting, but it gave me no help.

"Dad, take care of yourself," I said, doing my best to end the conversation on a positive note.

"I will, honey. You too."

"Goodbye, Dad."

"Bye, honey."

⚬◈⚬

Tara's call obviously hadn't been the one Daniel anticipated. When the phone rang, instead of Tara's voice, he'd expected to hear Christina's, even though her promised call was now eleven hours late. After hanging up with Tara, he went to the window and gazed outside. The rain had started again. Which perfectly reflected the gloom descending upon him.

It had been so long since he'd spoken with Tara that he hardly recognized her voice. And even this brief conversation violated the agreement with his ex-wife, which prohibited all communication with his former family. In exchange, his ex-wife had consented to a quick, uncomplicated financial settlement. He was very lucky in that regard—she'd been intent on a rapid and thorough dissolution. In short, she took their home and daughters, and nothing more. Which was a lot, but nowhere near what she could have ultimately gotten, especially materially.

In a way, she'd made it too easy on him. By stipulating no contact, she provided him no choice except to focus on himself. To devote all his energy toward fashioning a new life. Enabling him to put aside pretty much all the pain he'd caused others, especially Tara.

Not that he wasn't in substantial pain himself. Little seemed to be going well lately. He'd looked forward to the baseball practice, which had to be canceled. Christina had essentially rejected him and was continuing to do so by not phoning. He'd shown little or no progress in his quest to reduce his nocturnal escapades. And now, Tara reinforced all the negative feelings he had of himself by reminding him of his failure as a father and a husband.

He thought about Tara. About how considerate she was. About how her phone call had been much more about him than herself. About how she wondered what they could've done to have helped him.

And in what way had he reciprocated all these years? By selfishly getting caught up in his own needs and desires. By single-mindedly roaming the streets of L.A., and now San Francisco.

He glanced at the phone again. What a fool he was for expecting Christina to call. For harboring even the slightest hope that she, a street girl, could help him toward a new life.

He looked out the window once more and was surprised when the sun, at least briefly, peeked through the clouds.

⟡

"The Bears and the 49ers," Daniel spoke earnestly into the phone. "One of the oldest and best rivalries in pro football. Plus, San Francisco is a great place to be on Thanksgiving weekend."

"Especially if the Bears win," declared the male voice on the other end.

"We'll see to that," Daniel quipped.

"You promise?"

"That and good seats and a nice hotel."

Daniel was sitting in the sports tour company office a couple of days after Tara's phone call. The man he was talking with represented an athletic club in Chicago that offered tours for Chicago sports teams' fans. In past years, Daniel had arranged trips for them to see the Cubs play in Phoenix, the White Sox in New York, and the Bulls in New Orleans. This would be the first Bears excursion Daniel had planned—for this or any other organization.

"I'll send you a prospectus," Daniel went on.

"We'll need a good price."

"Haven't I always gotten you one in the past?"

"Yes," the guy admitted.

Daniel felt confident he'd made the sale. Since coming to San Francisco, he'd made several sales, even more than he'd become accustomed to making in L.A. In fact, this was the only part of his life here that had gone well lately.

"I expect the Bears to be in first place and undefeated when you get here on Thanksgiving," Daniel said with mock seriousness.

"Count on it," the guy affirmed.

ᴇᴏᴊᴇ

"What do you think?" Christina asked animatedly as the sounds of light jazz began from a large black tape player she had brought.

"I think we should dance." Daniel's smile barely expressed his utter excitement at seeing her.

Other than a brief giggle, she ignored his suggestion. Instead, she moved the tape player off the bed onto the floor. He could only shake his head at the improbability that he was again sitting in the same chair in the identical hotel room that they had rented for their only other extended time together, three weeks earlier.

She'd already completed a routine similar to the one she performed then. She'd gone to the window and opened it a little. Following a brief look outside, she went to the door and chain-locked it. Next, she inspected the carpet, walls, and bedding. He'd noticed that all her movements were quick and purposeful.

Now she sat down on the bed and began to mix ingredients into her brown pipe. Again, she used a hairpin as a blender. Once the pipe was ready, she placed it on a nightstand and got up to straighten the cushion on a chair. She turned on the TV and, like three weeks before, channel surfed. Nothing appealed to her, so she turned it off and sat back down on the bed. She kept time to the music for a few seconds by waving her left hand in front of her.

"Sorry about last week," she frowned. "I should've warned you . . . I'm very good at losing things. Especially phone numbers."

"You're forgiven."

"But I'm very good at finding things, too," she smiled. "Lots of practice."

He grinned at her explanation. And at the recollection of her excitement at reaching him by phone about an hour earlier. She'd also seemed excited to see him at her regular spot, minutes later. There she'd informed him that she finally found the card with his phone number, tucked inside a rarely used pocket of a pair of her jeans.

"So, you approve of the way I spent the money you *loaned* me?" she inquired as a piano solo on her jazz tape reached a crescendo.

"How did you spend it?" he puzzled.

"The tape player, silly." She nodded toward it. "And a bunch of old tapes."

"Nice."

"You think I did good?"

"Yes."

"Thanks," she said, taking a drag from her pipe. "Plus, I can pay you back every dollar I owe you. With interest."

"You must've been with some very generous people," he replied without much enthusiasm.

"Very generous," she confirmed.

She took several twenties from her backpack and put them beside her on the bed. She inhaled from her pipe again and leaned back against the same pillow she'd used the last time. Like then, he watched her closely, observing that she wore her hair in braids this time, giving her an even more youthful appearance.

"The music isn't all I bought," she announced.

"Oh?"

"I bought a Scrabble game."

"A what?"

"A Scrabble game," she repeated eagerly, taking a small box out of her backpack and putting it on the bed. It was red and white, with Scrabble spelled out across it. "Ever play?"

"A little," he answered, recalling his wife insisting that they use the game as an educational tool for their daughters.

"Want to?"

"Now?"

"Sure. I used to play with my father," she said wistfully.

"He any good?"

"He taught me when I was a kid," she avoided his question. "By the time I was eight or nine, he couldn't beat me."

"Then what chance do I have?"

"Well, I haven't played in years," she lamented, again wistfully.

"So, you're rusty."

"Shouldn't I be?"

"Well, then let's make a bet," he proposed playfully.

"What do you want to bet?" She both sounded and looked intrigued. When they first entered the room, making a bet was the last thing on his mind. He rubbed his chin, thinking. While she took another drag from her pipe, he glanced at the money, still on the bed beside her.

"How about," he began while moving over to the bed and sitting down, "you win, we forget the loan? You keep the money."

"And if you win?"

"Already told you. Your music makes me want to dance."

"Doesn't seem like much of a prize for you. A dance."

"That's how sure I am of winning," he playfully challenged.

"We'll fucking see." She stuck out her tongue at him while lifting the lid off the Scrabble box.

⌖

"472 to 158."

It had become apparent long before Daniel—as mutually-agreed-upon scorekeeper—meekly announced the final tally, that he was badly overmatched. Her concentration amazed him. So did her skill and vocabulary. She'd used words like onyx, zonal, and squalor. For the last one, because the "s" pluralized "fort," already on the board, the "q" was on a double-letter score, the "o" landed on a triple-word score, and the usage of all seven of her letters earned a 50 point "bingo" bonus, she received 136 points.

"Would you like to keep score?" he asked her at one juncture.

"No, you're doing just fine," she answered as if scorekeeping was his only purpose in the game.

He noticed that while they played, she left her pipe on the night-stand. He also noticed that she seemed calm throughout the game, in sharp contrast to her earlier state, when she buzzed around during her routine of making room preparations. Only when they stopped playing did she reach for her pipe and take another drag.

"Nice game," he praised.

"Thanks."

She inhaled again. And again. After still another drag, she got off the bed, went over to her tape player, and turned up the volume. The same piano solo of earlier was playing.

"Sorry you didn't win your dance," she teased while returning to the bed.

"Me too."

"I'd be happy to give you a rematch. Double or nothing."

"Next time," he begged off.

"Promise?"

"I promise."

"Maybe you'd like a consolation prize this time," she smiled.

She got up from the bed and went over to her tape player again. She ejected the jazz tape and replaced it with another tape. Soft romantic music began. Then she took off her jeans, treating him to the sight of yellow panties, which nicely complemented the olive-green top she had on. He'd been right about his speculation of three weeks earlier—her legs *were* as slim as her upper body. Which, to him, in no way diminished her appeal.

"What're you doing?" he asked, a little rattled.

"Isn't it fucking obvious?"

"What'll that prove?"

"That there's more to me than a brilliant mind," she giggled.

He chuckled uneasily. He scratched his head and frowned. Like their other time in this room, something told him to go slow with her, that easy intimacy might not be his best choice.

"I suppose there's a penalty for leaving early again tonight," he said, trying to change the subject.

"Bad sport," she accused.

"What do you mean?"

"Just because you lost at Scrabble, you want to leave."

"Scrabble has nothing to do with it," he stated with some firmness.

"No, no penalty tonight." She sat back down on the bed.

"How come?"

"You've already been generous enough."

"As generous as those other people?" he questioned pointedly while glancing at the twenties still on the bed, and the tape player.

She didn't reply. Instead, she took another drag from her pipe. And another. He looked at the Scrabble game beside her.

"I plan to do a lot better next time," he declared. "Maybe even beat you."

"I fucking doubt it," she disputed.

His departure was rapid, probably because he realized that if he hesitated, he'd end up doing what he'd decided not to do.

The New York Mets pitcher, a tall, lanky right-hander, wound up and fired a fastball. The San Francisco Giants batter, a chunky lefty, swung and belted a drive to deep center field. Most of the crowd, including Daniel and Alfredo, rose from their seats and cheered lustily. The noise and excitement ended quickly, however, when the Mets center fielder drifted back near the wall and caught the ball. It was the third out of the inning, and the teams changed sides.

"It is almost a home run," Alfredo enthused.

"Close," Daniel concurred.

The two of them sat back down. It was a cool early-April afternoon at Candlestick Park, home of the Giants. This was Daniel and Alfredo's first outing as big and little brother. Robert Lawson hadn't been fibbing when he said he knew the agency director. A brief meeting and some simple paperwork qualified Daniel as an official "big brother."

Daniel arranged choice seats for the game through his company—near the third-base dugout, where the Giants players were stationed. Both he and Alfredo were wearing their Orioles caps. Daniel had actually invited Lawson to join them, but he was busy going to a movie with one of his three "little brothers."

"Coach?" Alfredo grinned shyly at Daniel.

"Yes, Alfredo."

"It make me happy to be your little brother."

"It makes me happy, too."

Daniel smiled at him as he spoke. He liked the way Alfredo looked, his Orioles cap, and long wavy dark hair a positive addition to his large head and husky frame. The boy seemed very much at home here, and Daniel was glad he had suggested this for their initial outing.

"I worry about one thing, Coach," Alfredo frowned as the Giants pitcher, also right-handed, warmed up for the next inning.

"What, Alfredo?"

"Because you are my big brother, that you will still be my coach."

"I'll still be your coach," Daniel grinned and patted him on the back.

⋅⊙⋅

Daniel did do better when he and Christina next played Scrabble the following week. But not *much* better. Instead of losing to her by 314 points, he lost by only 256.

Bob Marley and reggae were the evening's musical entertainment from her black tape deck in the center of the floor. She'd also brought an old faded-red dog-eared Scrabble dictionary, acquired at a garage sale. So that, according to her, they could confirm that the words they used were actual words. To make the game, she explained, "nice and official."

They'd gotten the same room for the third consecutive time. Once they'd taken the Scrabble letters off the board and put them back into the box, he moved from beside her on the bed, over to his regular chair. Predictably, she reached for her pipe—which she'd let lay on the nightstand the entire game—and took a couple of quick drags.

For the first time in his presence, she wore a dress. Although it wasn't fancy—light-blue, ankle-length, and likely a relic from the psychedelic era, which reputedly started in San Francisco—it did give her a touch of distinction that he hadn't observed before. Especially with the embellishment of turquoise earrings, similar-colored necklace, and sparkling silvery bracelets that she had on.

"You look like an angel," he praised as she turned off the bright light next to the bed.

"Me an angel?" she replied thoughtfully. "'Fraid not in this life."

She got up from the bed, went to the window, and looked outside. Possibly she spotted someone or something familiar because she stood there gazing for a full minute. Then she returned to the bed.

"I suppose you'll be leaving early again tonight," she spoke quietly while picking up her pipe once more.

"It's not early," he differed. Previously that evening, he had the same inner dialogue about staying that he had on their prior two occasions here. "It's almost midnight."

"Must be something wrong with you," she challenged, rolling up a sleeve on her dress.

"There's plenty wrong with me."

"You know what I fucking mean. Are you able to . . . ?"

"Much too often," he cut her off.

"What the fuck does that mean?"

"For another time," he sidestepped while getting up from his chair.

Like the week before, his exit was speedy. But he couldn't escape that light-blue dress and her angelic appearance. The image of her remained etched in his mind as he departed the hotel and headed on the sidewalk toward his car. Along the way, he passed two women, both attractive, but neither one made any impact.

Besides Christina's image, he also experienced a lot of confusion. Why, like the prior two times, had he been so quick to leave? Why didn't he begin to force himself to stay longer, to find out what, if anything, there really was between them, other than some initial attraction? After all, he'd become aware that his hopes for her, for them, were growing by the day.

Exactly what did he see in her aside from a comely light-blue dress and an angelic look? Sure, he found her appealing. Sure, he viewed her as a possible way out of his obsessive behavior. But there was more. Much more. Wasn't he starting to believe that she could provide his life meaning, far beyond the morass it had been? How stupid of him, though. How could he even be thinking about expecting all this from a street girl?

Yet the image of her in that light-blue dress remained long after he got into his car and drove off.

Chapter Six

"One more out," Daniel stated hopefully while sitting beside Robert Lawson in the third-base dugout.

"Yeah," Lawson grumbled. "'Cept look who it is."

Daniel grimaced as he watched a big kid, who already had three hits in the game and four runs-batted-in, stride arrogantly to home plate at the same baseball field at which Daniel had been attending practices. About fifty spectators sat in the grandstand next to the field. Three players, not currently in the game, jabbered nervously near Daniel and Lawson in the dugout. Daniel peered tensely through twilight fog, at the scoreboard, which showed the Orioles leading the White Sox eight to seven in the bottom of the sixth, the final inning of their first game of the season

"Wish we had somewhere to put him," Lawson lamented.

Daniel shared his sentiment. An intentional walk could be a possible strategy. Except that the bases were already loaded and the tying run would be forced in. Also, the next batter, another big kid, was a good hitter too. So, they might as well take their chances with this kid.

"Maybe he'll hit it at someone," Daniel muttered.

Lawson nodded. A cold breeze was blowing in from right field, and Daniel zipped up the black windbreaker he wore above his green shirt with orange Oriole insignia. Before the game, Lawson had handed out shirts to him and all the players.

The familiar "Hey, batter batter, hey, batter batter" refrain began as the Orioles pitcher, a left-hander, wound up and fired. The pitch came in high. The big kid, also a lefty, swung and slugged a liner to right field, the position Alfredo was playing. The ball seemed to tail in the breeze. Alfredo ran to his left, his glove hand, and reached out as the ball dropped toward the turf. The ball landed in his glove. Daniel felt ecstatic—the Orioles' first game of the season was a win. Then he saw that the ball had fallen from Alfredo's glove and rolled behind him.

Daniel heard himself groan. The tying run scored, followed closely by the winning run. The Orioles had lost, nine to eight.

The White Sox players celebrated with loud cheering, backslapping, and high-fives. Daniel watched Alfredo, head bowed, trudge off the field and sit down by himself on a bench far down the right-field foul line. He didn't even bother to pick up the dropped ball.

Daniel trotted toward him. The White Sox banter was still audible, although the breeze masked its volume. At the bench, Daniel sat down beside Alfredo, slumped over. He put an arm around him.

"I am sorry, Coach. I make us lose."

"No, Alfredo. You didn't make us lose."

"But I drop the ball."

"It was a tough play, Alfredo. The wind . . ."

"But the ball, it hit right here, Coach." The boy pointed to the pocket of his glove, where the ball landed.

"There'll be other chances, Alfredo."

Pressing against his shoulder, Daniel encouraged him to get up. Together, Daniel's arm still around him, they headed back toward the third-base dugout. The White Sox cheering had finally stopped.

∙❧∙

"What do you think our chances are of getting this same hotel room four times in a row?" Daniel, sitting in his regular chair, asked.

"About fucking zero," Christina answered. "The same as you beating me at Scrabble."

He laughed. In truth, by his calculation, her equation wasn't entirely accurate. No question, he had no chance of beating her at Scrabble. But continuing to get the same hotel room? Indeed, only minutes earlier, he had to offer the desk clerk a bribe—a ten-dollar tip—to entice him to switch a pre-paid reservation from this room to one down the hall.

Despite their arriving only five minutes before, she was well underway with her room preparations. A lamp badly required new placement, and the bed needed to be pushed squarely against the wall. Chamber music was that night's chosen concert, once she'd positioned her tape player in its usual spot in the center of the floor.

"You think we could do something different sometime?" he asked straightforwardly as she paused to survey her work.

"You mean like you taking off your clothes and me taking off my dress. And everything else?" She stuck out her tongue at him.

He gulped a little. He did glance at her dress briefly, though. It was brown, matching her eyes, and much more current than the light-blue one from last time. It was also much shorter—knee-length—and reconfirmed how thin her legs were.

Apparently satisfied with her room alterations, she sat down on the bed, took her pipe from her backpack, and began to ready it. When she crossed her legs, he felt an immediate stirring. She wasn't going to make things easy for him.

"What if we went out to dinner?" he tried to keep on track.

"What?"

"Go out to dinner," he stated more firmly.

"Now?"

"No. Maybe next week."

"You mean like . . . go out on a date?"

"Yeah. Like, go out on a date."

"A dinner date?" She cocked her head and touched her ear as if not hearing right.

"Yeah. A dinner date."

"Well," she retorted abruptly, "with my pathetic appetite, we'd be wasting our time."

"Then what about a movie? Or a walk in the park? Things normal people do."

"You haven't been paying attention," she scolded. "I don't fucking want to be normal."

Clearly, he was making no progress, so he didn't reply. She finished readying her pipe and took her first drag. She breathed it in deeply and took another. Sighing contentedly, she reached over and put her pipe on the nightstand. In the process, her dress slid up, presenting a fuller view of her legs. This time, a complete wave passed through him.

"Want to play Scrabble?" she offered, extracting the game from her backpack.

"Definitely," he responded, eager to shift his focus off her.

"I've got an idea." She gazed up at him. "Something different we could do."

"What?" he questioned a bit guardedly, aware of how unpredictable he found her.

"On Thursday night. You'll just have to come find out."

He rubbed his face, wondering what she had in mind.

⚜

Christina Lambeau usually lingered in a hotel room until noon. Sometimes, after arranging a late checkout, she even stayed beyond one or two. But the next morning, she left before ten because she had a lot to do. And besides, for some reason, she felt restless.

Daniel, as customary, had not spent the night. Nor did he make any advances, even though the way he gazed at her suggested that he wanted to. Her earlier insinuation—that there was something wrong with him—made perfect sense. Also, he was probably married or had a family or girlfriend stashed somewhere. He did surprise her, though, by agreeing to play a second game of Scrabble before he left, for which she rewarded him by purposely keeping her margin of victory down below 200 points.

First, after getting outside the hotel and encountering a brisk morning, she hit a couple of rummage sales. For less than ten bucks, she found two dresses and complementing accessories. Truth was, almost her entire wardrobe was gotten from rummage sales, garage sales, or thrift shops.

Next stop was Grandma's, to drop off her purchases and yesterday's clothes, and fill her backpack with what she needed for the rest of the day. From Grandma, an old Slavic woman to whom she was in no way related, she "rented" a small corner of a tiny studio apartment, in exchange for running errands like grocery shopping and picking up meds. So, as she had insisted to Daniel, she was no "bag lady," at least regarding any implication of being homeless.

The downtown public library was her regular late-afternoon, early-evening haunt. She had a standard routine—newspaper room to music department to literature room, spending about an hour in each place. The *San Francisco Chronicle* was her newspaper of choice because of its witty columnists. Her tastes in music, of course, varied. Today she listened, via earphones, to Scott Joplin—a jazz composer from the early twentieth century—and to a little-known rap artist who'd been shot dead only weeks before.

Her tastes varied in literature too. Although she loved being surrounded by all the masters, from Dostoevsky to Mann, she'd recently been drawn to a street writer, Charles Bukowski. But today, she forsook him for an unfinished novel by the existentialist, Albert Camus. Not easy material, although she'd been able to get into it because the main character reminded her of Daniel. Externally he seemed sure of himself, yet underneath she sensed inner turmoil and something else she couldn't quite identify.

Once she left the library, she normally stopped for something to eat, usually at a market. Next, she scored her evening's stash from a favorite dealer. Then she often took a walk. Since the brisk morning had turned into a warm afternoon and night, she knew a little exercise would feel good before she assumed her post against the apartment building wall.

She liked her neighborhood. Despite its reputation for danger, she felt safe here. What she valued most was the prevailing attitude of live and let live. She could go wherever she wanted and do whatever she pleased without anyone intruding.

Up ahead, as she walked, she spotted the large pink wall surrounding the building where she landed her first job soon after arriving in San

Francisco nearly a decade earlier. Unfortunately, that job became the first in succession lost to a growing drug habit. The building was home to about a hundred memory-care patients. She became an assistant to the Activity Director there.

The large pink wall reminded her of her favorite duty—reading to the residents. And especially how she'd begin by reciting one of her favorite nursery rhymes, Humpty Dumpty, and describing his disastrous fall. After she finished that and a few fairy tales, the residents would applaud loudly. Some even came up to her to shake hands or offer a hug.

The memory of all that made her smile now. Too bad the smile didn't last. She thought about the night ahead. She hoped that one of her steadies would show, but if one didn't—which was more likely--she'd have to deal with a stranger. One who'd make her do things she didn't want to do. Unlike when she was with Daniel and could play Scrabble.

Chapter Seven

"I believe that in a former life, I was a nun," the graying fiftyish woman stated. Heavy-set and wearing a frumpy brown pantsuit, she was standing at her chair, addressing about 20 or 25 people sitting in the circle she was part of.

"What makes you say that?" probed the leader of the group, a balding man of about sixty, seated approximately 20 feet to her left. He had cleared his throat before speaking.

"Whenever possible," the woman replied tentatively, "I've always avoided sex. During my marriage, and before and after."

Daniel glanced sidelong at Christina, seated next to him, but she continued to gaze straight ahead at the woman, who was directly across from them. It was Thursday night, and a reincarnation meeting was the "something different" Christina had in mind for them to do. A meeting taking place in a dark, drab and musty community center near Market Street.

"Maybe you're not attracted to men," the leader speculated.

"I've tried with women, too," the woman admitted softly, sounding ashamed. "Didn't work."

"What do you remember about your life as a nun?"

"Nothing. But I've always had an affinity for the elements of religion. The words to prayers and hymns were easy to memorize. Like I knew them already."

"As a nun, you were Catholic, I assume."

"I guess so," she shrugged.

"And yet you believe in reincarnation now?"

"Not so strongly as I'd like."

"So, you're here to explore?" the leader pressed on once he cleared his throat again.

"I am," the woman acknowledged, dropping her head.

"Thank you," the leader spoke dismissively while glancing at his watch.

The woman sat down. The leader got up. Daniel, feeling restless, looked at his watch too. They'd been here two hours.

"Same time next week," the leader proclaimed and summarily headed for the exit.

Christina got up, and so did Daniel. Others remained or began milling around the room. Christina led him to the exit. Outside, the night had become a bit foggy. A bicyclist rode by and waved to them. Daniel suspected that the guy knew Christina.

"Are you like that woman?" he asked as they neared his car. "Here to explore?"

"Much more than that," she answered frankly. "For me, reincarnation is like . . . a religion."

"Why?"

"It's my best chance," she declared resolutely, "to try and get things right."

He glanced at her thoughtfully. They reached his car, and he unlocked the passenger door for her. She got in, and he went around to the other side. As he drove off, he could feel her looking at him in the dark.

"How'd you like the meeting?" she asked.

"Well, I haven't had much exposure to that stuff. And besides, I'm more a meat and potatoes guy."

He could feel her turn away and look straight ahead at the road.

⚬⟨⊙⟩⚬

"You're playing better," Christina commented a few nights later as Daniel put away the final letters after they'd finished another Scrabble game.

"You think there's hope for me?"

"Some," she winked. "More in Scrabble than in other things."

"What's that supposed to mean?" he feigned anger while pretty sure of her intent, then wishing he hadn't suggested she elaborate.

He moved from next to her on the bed to his regular chair in their same hotel room. She was right about his playing better. Even though she still clobbered him by no fewer than 238 points, he did have two very successful sequences. He bingoed with "derived," scoring 86 points, 50 of which were a bonus for using his entire rack of letters. Later he challenged one of her plays, "shafter," also a possible bingo. When they checked her dog-eared dictionary, the word wasn't there, requiring her to both remove it from the board and lose her turn.

"That woman at the meeting," she said, eyes twinkling. "She kind of reminded me of you."

"How?" he acted innocent, though fully aware that she was elaborating on her same theme.

"How she always avoided sex."

Growing a little tired of this subject, both because she kept bringing it up and because he was becoming more and more conflicted over whether he should finally make advances, he twisted uneasily in his chair. Fortunately, a series of car horns honked on the street outside, diverting her attention. She got up, went to the window, and shut it, reducing the noise.

"Now that we're dating," he said, trying to change the subject before she could get back to it.

"Dating? I don't call going to a reincarnation meeting much of a date."

"Maybe not. But still a date."

"If you insist," she relented, looking and sounding bored. She returned to the bed and took a long drag from her pipe.

"Anyway, now that we're dating . . . I was thinking maybe we should go steady."

"Go . . . steady," she repeated slowly as if she hadn't heard right. "You don't mean like teenagers."

He nodded slightly and felt a little embarrassed. She took a couple more quick drags. There was further horn honking outside, but she ignored it.

"Back in high school," he explained softly, no less embarrassed, "I never had a steady girlfriend. I'm afraid I was sorta backward."

"You're serious about all this," she said, shaking her head in obvious disbelief. "You don't want me seeing other people."

"Right," he confirmed shyly.

"How would I survive?" She looked perplexed.

"I'd take care of you. You've already admitted you don't eat much."

"Aren't you forgetting something?" She glanced at her pipe.

"I'll take my chances," he replied more firmly.

Static started coming from her tape player. She got off the bed, went over to the tape player, and shook it. The static stopped immediately. She went back to the bed and inhaled deeply from her pipe.

"Where would I stay?" she asked.

"We'd find a place?"

"We?" She raised her eyebrows. "You mean we'd live together?"

"Yes."

"And you'd pay all my expenses!"

"Yes."

"Including my pipe?"

"Including your pipe."

"But why?" She looked perplexed again.

"I told you," he chuckled. "I've never gone steady before."

"I'm fucking being serious," she scolded. "Why should you spend all this money on me?"

"I guess because . . . I want you," he answered earnestly.

"But you can have me, Mr. Meat and Potatoes," she said, shaking her head in disbelief once more, "almost any time you want me. For the mere price of a hotel room."

"That's not the way I want you."

She shook her head yet another time. She took several more rapid drags from her pipe. Then, as if it had no answers for her confusion, she put it on the far end of the nightstand.

"Does this mean you're going to finally spend the night with me?" she said, perking up. "Tonight."

"If you accept my proposal," he replied thoughtfully while rubbing his cheek.

"You expect me to decide right now?"

"No."

"But you won't stay until I do. Not even to fucking try it out."

"Not even to try it out," he responded decisively.

"I'll need some time."

"Take all the time you need."

She grabbed her pipe off the nightstand and inhaled deeply again. He got up from the chair, went over to the bed, and, for the first time since their initial encounter in this room, he kissed her. Not on the forehead as he did then, but on the lips. Gently at first, then more ardently. She was resistant, pulling back slightly. Which only encouraged him to kiss her more passionately. He felt a wave pass through him. Maybe he should stay. No question he wanted to. Possibly slightly less because he wanted her than because he loved being with her.

He finally pulled away. He got off the bed. Without looking back at her or saying a single word, he went to the door, opened it, and stepped out into the hallway. He expected her to say something, perhaps hoped that she would encourage him to stay.

She didn't, however, and he had no choice except to head down the corridor and out of the hotel.

⋆⟨◉⟩⋆

"Dumb me," Daniel, a little embarrassed, admitted. "Asked a girl to go steady."

"That street girl you spoke of?" Lawson conjectured.

"Yep."

"You move quick," Lawson commented, although Daniel wasn't sure it was praise or criticism.

The two of them were sitting at a table in a downtown San Francisco sports bar, nearing the end of a dinner, their first one together. Numerous TVs were scattered throughout, showing various games. Several patrons watching a hockey match cheered a player scoring a goal. Lawson had suggested this place because it was close to where he worked as director of a legalized medical marijuana center. Daniel was fascinated by Lawson's position, and it had provided most of their conversation so far.

Lawson's appetite amazed him too. In fact, after Lawson had finished three courses already, their waiter delivered a huge slice of pie ala mode, and Lawson was busy polishing it off as well. Daniel also marveled at Lawson's skill in wielding knife, fork, and spoon with his single hand. Switching utensils dexterously, almost as if they were batons and he was a talented drum major in a marching band, he cut the pie with his knife, ate a bite with his fork, then scooped some ice cream with the spoon.

"How's your kid?" Lawson inquired with his mouth practically full. "He get over dropping that ball?"

"He will. Took him to a Giants game. We're planning a movie this week."

"Ever think about adopting?" Lawson asked a question Daniel wasn't expecting.

"Not with my . . . legal problems," he answered uncomfortably.

"Kid his age, they can't be too choosy."

"I suppose you know the adoption people too."

"They're right across the street from the Big Brothers," Lawson winked.

Daniel grinned. A player in a baseball game on TV hit a home run, and several bar patrons applauded. Throughout the meal, Daniel had trouble not glancing at Lawson's stub of a right arm. To limit his glances, he tried to focus on Lawson's strikingly white teeth, which contrasted starkly with his black skin. He also couldn't help noticing the bright red tie Lawson was wearing, causing Daniel to wonder how he managed to tie it with only one hand.

"Things work out with your girl," Lawson noted, "that'll help too. They like couples."

"So," Daniel spoke with lightness in his tone, "yesterday I was Alfredo's coach, and today I'm his big brother. Tomorrow you'll have me being his father. *You* move pretty quick yourself."

Lawson stopped eating for a second, threw back his head, and laughed heartily.

Chapter Eight

"Kneel on the bed, cunt," the shithead commanded. "Ass in the air. Facing me."

"Me facing you?" Christina whimpered. "Or my ass?"

"Your ass. Right now, or I'll fucking slice it up."

She believed him. In fact, he'd already poked the sharp end of his long switchblade into her butt, and it had hurt like hell. He now stood behind her, holding the knife in one hand---pressed against her right side---and her long hair with the other hand. The two of them were in the very seedy motel room he had rented for them about an hour earlier. Other than a single pink sock on her left foot, she was completely naked.

The shithead—thirtyish, short, wiry, a surly expression altering an otherwise nondescript face—tried to shove her toward the bed. He had trouble moving her, though, because her body was inert with fear. With the fist holding the knife, he punched her hard in the mouth. She emitted several muffled sobs, which accompanied her labored, coerced path onto the bed.

"Now fucking do as you're told," he ordered. "Or next time it'll be the knife."

"One condition," she whimpered again.

"Hey, cunt," he seethed, pulling her hair harder and sticking the blade of the knife into her skin again. "You're in no position to negotiate."

"Then cut me," she uttered a little more firmly.

That seemed to slow the shithead down. At least he didn't speak for several seconds. Although she was facing away from him, she could smell his garlicky breath, and it disgusted her. Or maybe it was just his general presence.

"What's the condition, cunt?" he relented a little.

"Everyone uses a rubber," she surprised herself with an even firmer response. "Especially for *that*."

"No problemo." His reply was laced with sarcasm. "Don't wanna catch nothin' ass-fucking a tramp like you."

He pushed her higher up on the bed. She heard him unzip his pants, and she grimaced with apprehension. She glanced behind her briefly and saw him fumbling with a condom and some sort of greasy lubricant.

A small dark spider climbed up the wall beyond the bed, and she tried to focus on it to blot out thoughts of what was about to occur. No easy task. Not with the ringing in her mouth from the shithead's punch, his garlicky breath, and the sense of humiliation she felt looming over her. And who knew what the guy would do to her afterward?

"Raise your ass some more," he instructed.

She attempted to comply. No point fighting the shithead now. She concentrated on spreading her legs and leaning forward on her elbows so that her butt was elevated above the rest of her frame, but her agility failed her, and she fell on her face.

"C'mon, cunt," he chastised belittlingly. "Do it!"

Using her hands and arms, she tried to hoist herself back up. She started trembling, however, and moved very slowly and carefully. Any second, she expected to feel the sharp sting of the switchblade piercing her butt once more. Finally, she managed to raise herself into some type of stable position.

"Nice," the shithead surprised her with a positive remark.

She went back to the spider. Anything to erase the mental picture of her ass sticking up in the air. She could feel the shithead right behind her and anticipated his penetration. She gritted her teeth, and when it came, she heard herself wince in pain.

As the shithead pumped away, she watched the spider take a circuitous path toward the ceiling. It paused at a darkened spot near where the wall and ceiling met. The guy was breathing hard behind her. And then, luckily much quicker than she could hope for, he finished and zipped up.

What would happen next? She could almost feel the sensation of his knife cutting her butt. She didn't turn around to see what he was doing, though. She didn't dare turn around to see what he was doing. Instead, she watched the spider resume its trek, now onto the ceiling.

Then the shithead was gone. At least that was her assumption because she heard the room door open and close. Still, she didn't turn around right away. When she finally did, she sighed. The shithead *was* gone.

Aware that she was continuing to tremble, she methodically struggled off the bed and began to make her way over to chain-lock the door.

⋅❦⋅

How much Christina despised the shithead and never wanted to see him again was how much she liked and hoped to keep seeing Uncle Harold, whose apartment she woke up in three mornings later. After lying in bed alone for nearly an hour, she got up and made herself breakfast. Toast, coffee, orange juice, and soft-boiled eggs—items she seldom ate elsewhere.

She put everything onto a tray and carried it into the living room, her favorite place in the apartment. Furnishings were elegant. But, more obvious, it resembled a museum. Uncle Harold being an art dealer, beautiful paintings covered the walls—ranging from Alexander Calder to Pablo Picasso.

She sat down in her favorite chair, a late-nineteenth-century heirloom. The phone rang. She didn't even stir since she didn't have to answer it. In fact, she wasn't allowed to answer it, unless she wanted to risk not being able to see Uncle Harold anymore.

Normally she saw him about twice a month, usually on Friday nights. Like Grandma, he wasn't a blood relative. There were plenty of reasons for calling him Uncle Harold, though. Financially, he was consistently generous. He always treated her well, too, never requiring much of her, either physically or emotionally. And, during the couple of years she'd known him, his drugs had always been good. Plus—an added perk—after leaving for the weekend for his family home about fifty miles north of San Francisco—he let her stay as long as she wanted the next day. Provided, of course, that she did not answer his phone.

She sipped some orange juice. Then she tried a bite of toast. She winced immediately when a hard edge of the bread brushed her lip. The spot where the shithead punched her may have worsened. In the last day or so, she'd seen part of her lip change color twice, now turning a dark purple. Maybe it had become infected.

The pain made her think of the shithead again. How he reminded her of a pimp. Funny, she hadn't thought of that until now. Selfish, quick-tempered, abusive, controlling—he had all the characteristics.

Her one and only alliance with a pimp was a disaster. She'd recently gotten out of jail for drug possession and prostitution and was having trouble getting established again. Salvadore, like the shithead, had been a trick, and when he offered a place to live and steady drugs, she accepted.

Right from the start, she had no freedom. Salvadore dictated everything—her clothes, hairstyle, who she slept with. She'd simply gone from one prison to another. Despite winding up in essentially the same position as after her jail release, she was relieved when he got mad one day and kicked her out for refusing a trick.

She tried the soft-boiled eggs. They hurt her lip less than the toast. From Salvadore and the shithead, her thoughts switched to Daniel. Specifically, to his proposal. In truth, she hadn't considered it much. Sure, it was tempting, but why take it seriously? After all, she hardly knew him. And as she'd concluded before, like Uncle Harold, he probably had his own family stashed somewhere.

Also, he might turn into another Salvadore. Not a pimp, of course, but end up being someone who wouldn't give her any freedom. She'd have to escape. And wind up losing him and losing Uncle Harold too.

But would she have to lose Uncle Harold too? What if she merely "tried out" Daniel's proposal to see how it would work out, while at the same time continuing to see Uncle Harold? Why would Daniel need to find out? Too bad she knew the answer to all these questions—she never did anything halfway. She prided herself that when she gave her word on something, that's what she did.

She finished her breakfast, picked up the tray, and took it back to the kitchen. The phone rang again. This time it startled her.

⋅◦⟨◉⟩◦⋅

"Your lip looks terrible," Daniel exclaimed once they got out of the hotel elevator on their floor.

Christina ignored him, preferring instead to postpone any response until they got inside their room. But she knew he was right, having appraised her lip in a lobby mirror just before meeting him, and seeing that the shade of purple was even darker than at Uncle Harold's that morning. However, she did consider it a positive that they'd been able to rent their same room for the sixth consecutive time. As she unlocked their door, she could feel his warm breath on the back of her neck.

"So, what happened?" he spewed impatiently after slamming the door shut behind them.

"A shithead with a knife."

"Rape?"

"Not exactly. But close."

"I thought you were always careful."

"I blew it."

"You call the police?"

"Oh, fuck yes," she spewed back at him while sitting down on the bed. "Guess who'd wind up in jail. Again."

"Why didn't you call me?" he scolded.

"Not your problem. What the fuck could you do?"

"What I'm going to do now. Make sure you're okay."

"I'm okay. Except for my lip."

"Let me see."

She watched him approach the bed. He looked grim while standing over her. As he examined the wound and shook his head, she gazed into his eyes. She'd never realized they were that blue.

"I guess you don't have a regular doctor," he said.

"Good guess."

"We're going to an emergency room to see one."

"Not now," she disputed.

"Now."

"What about Scrabble?"

"It'll have to wait."

"What about my pipe?"

"It'll have to wait."

It was her turn to become grim. He moved to the door while she remained on the bed and thought about the new jazz tape that she had brought. And about the prospect of the awful emergency room, which would undoubtedly be crowded and noisy.

"One condition," she grudgingly relented, in her usual way.

"What?"

"One guess."

Of course, she knew that he knew that she would want him to spend the night. She'd made no secret of it before. She also knew that he would probably bring up his proposal.

"Any decision?" he asked, right on cue.

"About?" she replied, playing dumb.

"About going steady."

"I need more time."

"So, you won't go to the emergency room," he shrugged. "Unless I stay with you tonight."

"I won't."

"Then, I will."

⋅⟨❀⟩⋅

When they got back from the emergency room, a few blocks away, their hotel room was warm and stuffy. Almost by reflex, Christina took off the lavender top she had on and flung it angrily at a chair. She felt like also taking off the tan bra she wore, but she restrained herself.

She smelled food—likely from someone cooking down the hall— and she rushed to the window and noisily opened it. She went to her tape player and shoved in her jazz album, its high energy an especially good choice after how boring the emergency room had been. She'd brought her Scrabble set there, but it had been so crowded that they couldn't find room to play.

"What a waste," she exclaimed for probably the third time since they'd seen the doctor.

"Look, I'm sorry," Daniel replied, probably also for the third time. "At least we know your lip's not serious."

"I could have told you that," she retorted caustically while practically dive-bombing onto the bed. "Without spending three mother-fucking hours in that stupid place. Without my pipe."

"I think you just ID'd the problem," he said while sitting down in his regular chair.

"What?"

"Your pipe. You don't smoke, you don't have to be in rooms with guys with knives."

"But I do smoke." She picked up her pipe for emphasis.

"Maybe you should stop."

"Maybe I've tried!" She could hear the venom in her own voice. "Only about a zillion times. Fucking find my way blindfolded to every detox in this city."

"Where's all this leading?"

"You tell me," she muttered, waving her left arm, the non-pipe-holding one, in front of her. "You're the one with all the fucking answers."

She realized that she was swearing even more than she usually did, so she purposely forced herself to shut up and concentrate on preparing her pipe. Luckily, he didn't say anything right then either, because if he continued this line of reproach, she'd probably unleash another barrage. Wouldn't she have been justified, this being the first time he'd criticized her smoking? He didn't have that right, especially considering his proposal. Especially considering the awful time they'd just had in the emergency room.

"I won't hold you to your promise," she spoke softly, finally breaking the silence.

"About tonight? Or about going steady?"

"Both," she quickly replied.

Really, she meant only about tonight. She was still too angry to differentiate, though. Indeed, had he presented ten different options for her answer, she'd have probably affirmed all ten. The instant her response slipped out, she recognized her mistake.

"Are you sure?" he questioned, giving her a chance for retraction.

"I'm sure," she uttered, still too mad to waver. "If you're going to change the damn rules."

She wasn't sure he understood the intent of her last statement. She wasn't sure she understood, either. About the only thing she was sure of was that she'd finally managed to finish preparing her pipe. No doubt trying to calm herself and register disdain at his bringing up the topic of her smoking, she took a deliberately extended drag.

"I'm sorry," he admitted softly, surprising her. "I shouldn't be pushing you. I'm as frustrated as you about that miserable emergency room."

"You still don't have to stay."

What was she doing, pressing on like this? After all, he'd apologized. And she could tell by his sincere expression that he meant it. Then she recognized what she was doing—she was testing him.

"Do you want me to leave?" he asked again softly.

"I don't want you to stay," she answered, taking a couple more quick drags, "if you don't want to."

"I want to," he replied promptly.

What should she do now? Although she was still angry, he had apologized. And he'd stopped his attack on her smoking. And she really didn't want him to leave. Fortunately, the doctor they'd seen in the emergency room had provided a ready excuse for her to escape—an ointment for her lip. She took the tube it was in out of her backpack, raised it to signal Daniel, then ducked into the bathroom.

While using the medicine cabinet mirror to apply the medication, she grew more disturbed. She could see how skinny her upper body was. Didn't he gaze strangely at her while she pranced around the room in her tan brassiere? And, in a few minutes, when she got into bed for the first time with the first person she'd even remotely cared about in years, she'd have to reveal even more of herself. Funny how cavalier she'd always acted with everyone, he included. Except now, when it mattered, she felt very nervous and shy.

Not expecting this change in their routine, she'd put only a frumpy old nightgown into her backpack. Inappropriate for his first time to stay all night. Should she take off her jeans and get into bed in her underwear? Or should she brazenly take everything off and slip quickly beneath the sheets? Actually, she'd really prefer putting her top back on. But then she'd have to find it and probably give some type of excuse. Maybe she could get a clue what to do from him.

As she eased out of the bathroom, she could see that he was no help. He was in the same position she'd left him in—sitting in his chair, without having taken off a single stitch of clothing. Plus, he was right next to her top. She probably couldn't get to it even if she wanted to. And he was watching her.

No question, the next move was hers. Might as well get it over with. Taking a deep breath, she eased out of her jeans. Quickly, wearing only panties—also tan—and her bra, she slid into bed. Luckily, she'd left her pipe on the nightstand nearby, within reach. She grabbed it and took several rapid drags.

"You going to sit there all night?" she asked pointedly, trying to transfer some of her discomfort to him.

"I didn't bring any pajamas."

"As you may have fucking noticed," she countered sarcastically, "neither did I."

He shrugged. She watched him get up from the chair. He took off his jacket and shirt, placing each carefully on the chair, near her top. She realized that in the two months or so that they'd been acquainted, she'd never seen him in even the slightest state of undress. Which was a first for her, regarding any of her male companions.

"I like the way you look," she praised, much less angry.

"Thanks."

"Very distinguished."

"It's my gray hair."

"My father had gray hair," she sighed.

After removing his shoes and socks, he took off his pants and put them on the chair also. He turned off the only lights in the room and joined her in bed, wearing only boxers and a T-shirt. Once more, she could feel his warm breath, this time on her face. Her jazz tape had ended, and, other than occasional sounds from the street, the room was quiet.

She put her pipe back on the nightstand and rubbed his leg gently with her toes. He kissed her forehead lightly. Even in the dark, she could tell he was gazing at her face and body, and she hoped he wasn't repelled by her skinniness. She massaged his leg again, this time with the sole of her foot. His only response was another gentle kiss on the forehead. She edged her entire body against his, but he quickly moved away.

"You don't like me," she whispered.

"I'm crazy about you."

"I swear all the time. And you think I'm too skinny."

"I think you're perfect."

"Then why won't you make love?" She tried to nuzzle against him once more.

"I never agreed to make love," he said, inching away. "Only to spend the night."

"And nothing more?"

"I won't stand in line," he spoke firmly.

"Meaning?"

"Meaning I want to be different than the other men in your life."

"And if I agree to your proposal?"

"We can do whatever you say."

"Silly man," she muttered, reaching for her pipe again.

⋅◈⋅

"Hello," Daniel announced his waking as church bells sounded in the distance, ringing in the new dawn.

"Hello," Christina replied softly, again feeling his warm breath on her face.

"Time for me to go."

"I figured. Thank you."

"For what?" he questioned.

"For the way you are."

Surprisingly, she didn't feel disappointed that they hadn't made love during their first night together. Instead, she felt a sort of cozy warmth. No man had ever slept with her before without demanding sex.

The closest they had come was his waking her twice in the night by kissing her forehead. But both interludes had been brief. She had fallen quickly back to sleep each time, and she assumed he did too.

"One thing," she said. "Before you go."

"A penalty?" he asked. "For leaving early?"

"No," she smiled. "Your prize."

"Prize?"

"Yes."

"For what?" He looked confused.

"I already told you," she answered, getting up out of bed. "For the way you are."

She went to her tape player, ejected her jazz album, and replaced it with a nearby tape that she had a little trouble seeing in the scant light. Soft romantic music began. She motioned him to get out of bed and come to her.

He got up immediately. As he approached, she raised her arms into a slow-dance position. When he reached her, it became clear he understood, because he reciprocated, taking her right hand in his left and placing his other one above her waist, in the center of her back. Together, still dressed in only their underwear, they started to whirl around the room. She saw him smile, then heard him laugh.

"You didn't forget," he whispered in her ear.

"No."

"But I haven't come close to beating you at Scrabble. Wasn't that our bet?"

"Yes," she grinned. "But some things are more important than Scrabble."

The song ended, and she let go of him. He went over to the chair and the rest of his clothes. As he quickly dressed, she saw that he was still smiling. Another song began, but she could tell he wanted to leave. She moved to him anyway. Once he finished dressing by tying his shoes, he kissed her forehead again and briefly held her. Then he went rapidly to the door and, without looking back at her, opened it and was gone.

Instead of feeling relieved with being alone, as she virtually always did once a man left, she experienced an immediate emptiness. Normally she went back to sleep; however she knew right away that this morning she wouldn't be able to.

⋅⟨◉⟩⋅

Even though it was still barely dawn, Christina followed Daniel's lead by getting dressed. No sense lying in bed, with that empty feeling lingering. She quickly brushed her teeth, combed her hair, gathered her stuff, left the room, and checked out of the hotel.

Her first stop was a small neighborhood coffee shop, where she ordered a four-pancake breakfast. On the way there, she'd decided that if her thinness was why Daniel didn't want to make love to her, she'd eliminate that reason once and for all. Even if she had to force food down her throat.

While eating, she noticed that her lip didn't hurt. Evidently, the ointment was working. She laughed out loud—leave it to Daniel to make a medical emergency out of a bruised lip. But then maybe that was part of the attraction.

"Skinny is a thing of the past," she declared to herself, finishing the last bite.

The morning was cool and sunny. It was too early to shop for the old woman—the neighborhood grocery wouldn't be open yet. So, she opted to walk toward Union Square. She began to feel funny, though, observing all the businesspeople heading to work. She focused on the women, immaculately dressed in business attire. Maybe she should do some shopping when the department stores opened. Expand her wardrobe. Instead, she turned back.

Once the market opened, she shopped. On the way to delivering groceries to Grandma's, she passed by the pink wall, as she had a couple of weeks earlier. Like then, she thought about Humpty Dumpty, her first job in San Francisco, and reciting nursery rhymes and fairy tales to the building's memory-challenged residents. How about going inside and telling some stories for old times' sake? Maybe she would someday . . .

She arrived at Grandma's and dropped off the groceries. Time to do laundry. She gathered some of her clothes and put them in her backpack. During the walk to her favorite Laundromat, she passed in front of a bakery. Several large chocolate éclairs were displayed on a counter next to the window.

She went inside and bought the three largest ones. Back on the street, she began eating them. By the time she reached the Laundromat, she'd devoured all three.

"He's going to call me 'Fatty' before long," she said to herself, smiling.

Chapter Nine

Sitting next to Lawson in the first base dugout and nervously rubbing his hands together, Daniel watched Alfredo walk to home plate with a bat in his hands. The game was on the line. The Orioles trailed the Cubs 5-4 with two outs in the bottom of the sixth, the final inning. But the Orioles had the potential tying run on third and winning run on second.

"C'mon Alfredo," Daniel called out. "A good hit and we win."

The boy tapped his bat on home plate. The pitcher, a gangly red-headed right-hander, stared at Alfredo. He wound up and fired. Alfredo must have been pretty nervous too, not to mention eager, because he immediately fell into his old habit of stepping away from the pitch as he swung. The result was a weak dribbler, foul, outside of third base.

"C'mon Alfredo," Daniel encouraged, clapping his hands together. "Like we practiced."

The boy nodded. The gangly kid stared at him again. He fired another pitch. This time Alfredo's swing was even worse, his stepping away more pronounced, and he missed the ball badly.

He backed out of the batter's box and looked toward Daniel. Daniel got up, pretended to have a bat in his hands, and took an imaginary swing, trying to illustrate stepping into the pitch, not away from it. Alfredo nodded once more and took a practice swing himself, demonstrating the right technique. To quiet his nerves, Daniel paced through the dugout, behind Lawson.

"Hey, batter batter, hey, batter batter."

The redundant chatter, which of course, had recurred throughout the game, seemed louder than ever. Except now, Daniel was more affected by it because of his tension. In addition to pacing, he clapped his hands again, repeatedly.

The gangly kid delivered his next pitch. The ball headed for the low and outside part of the strike zone, a strategic place against a batter who'd already stepped away twice. But this time, Alfredo was ready. He stepped toward the pitch, not away from it. He hit a liner over the second baseman's head, into right-center field. The ball landed and skipped past the two outfielders attempting to converge on it, all the way to the fence. Both baserunners scored. The game was over; the Orioles had their first win of the season, 6 to 5.

All the Orioles rushed Alfredo as he stood near second base. High-fives and backslaps ensued. Even from the dugout, Daniel could see Alfredo's elation. But it was nowhere near the intensity of his own.

⋅◈⋅

"Notice something different about the way I look?" Christina asked while she and Daniel sat on the bed in their regular hotel room, drawing letters for their customary Scrabble game.

"Sure," he answered. "Your lip's much better."

It was true; her lip was much better. She'd examined it earlier that evening and found it only slightly discolored. But that's not what she had in mind with her question.

"Something else," she prodded.

"Your hair," he guessed. "Very pretty."

"Not my hair, silly."

She was getting impatient. She took a drag from her pipe, then stood up on the bed and did a little pirouette. Along with a matching blouse, she'd purposely worn her grayish-blue skirt because it flowed and was a size too big, making her look heavier than she was.

"Your outfit," he spoke admiringly. "Very, very nice."

Growing even more impatient, she put her hands on her hips. She was still standing up on the bed, directly in front of him. They'd been there around fifteen minutes, time enough for her to buzz around making her obligatory room preparations—window openings, adjusting wall pictures, carpet inspection—plus readying her pipe and inserting a tape into her tape player. This evening's concert featured classic show tunes.

"Don't you see how heavy I've gotten?" she scolded, pointing a finger at him. "Must've gained ten pounds."

"You've been eating."

"Like a horse."

"That mean we can start having dinner dates?" he winked. "Like *normal* people."

She chuckled and sat back down on the bed. It was his turn to go first in their Scrabble game, and she watched him study his letters. After briefly rotating them on his rack, he played the word "veil" on the board.

"Fourteen points," he announced, writing it down on the scorecard beside him. "I lead fourteen-nothing. I think it's the first time I've ever been ahead of you."

"And most likely the last," she chuckled again.

A new show tune began on her tape player, "Chicago, My Home Town," with Frank Sinatra singing. She took another drag from her pipe, this one a long one. Then she glanced repeatedly at her tape player.

"Anything wrong?" he asked.

"Well . . . that song."

"What about it?"

"Chicago *is* my hometown."

"Oh?"

"Lots of memories there," she spoke wistfully.

"Tell me."

"Let's play Scrabble," she avoided.

"Tell me," he insisted.

"Well," she said thoughtfully, sighing. "I wasn't supposed to end up like this."

"Like this?"

"Smoking dope in some cheap hotel room."

He frowned. She sighed once more. Neither of them spoke right away, as Frank Sinatra crooned away.

"Back in Chicago," she finally continued, aware of the melancholy in her voice, "my father used to take me to all kinds of science stuff. Museums and lectures. And expos at least once a month."

"Was he a scientist?"

"No. Just a science junkie. He loved discoveries. Especially medical ones."

"And you?"

"Ditto," she recalled clearly as if that part of her life took place yesterday. "We both wanted me to study science in college. I began applying for scholarships. And he'd put away some tuition money."

"So, what happened?"

"He died suddenly," she replied, even more sadly. "Heart attack. My last year of high school."

"I'm sorry . . . What about your mother?"

"Died years before. I was the only child of older parents."

He shook his head. She fiddled with the Scrabble letters in her rack, without paying any attention to them. She wished that she'd previewed the tape because if she had, she probably never would have played it.

"An uncle took me in," she went on. "Didn't work out. So instead of college, I came to San Francisco with a friend. I guess you can guess the rest."

He shrugged. He too fiddled with his letters. It looked to her like he was about to say something, but he didn't. She decided to introduce a slightly different subject, one that had been on her mind for some time.

"I told you about my family," she began. "You've never told me about yours."

"They're gone, too," he replied solemnly.

"Dead?"

"I pretty much am to them," he answered straightforwardly.

"Well, we have that much in common," she concluded, deciding not to probe further. "Besides Scrabble."

"I don't think we have Scrabble much in common," he smiled faintly. "Not the way you wallop me all the time."

She smiled faintly, too, acknowledging his attempted humor. But she wasn't quite ready to let the conversation slip into lightness. Frank Sinatra finally finished the song, and a new one, "Oklahoma," began.

"Long as we're being serious," she said, taking an extended drag from her pipe, "I was wondering something else."

"Yes?"

"Your proposal. Why is it so important to you that we go steady?"

"I told you. I never had a girlfriend in high school."

"But this isn't high school," she countered.

"I also told you I won't stand in line. I don't want to share you."

"Share me?" she responded emphatically. "How can you share what you've never had?"

"I guess," he answered tentatively, "I want all or nothing."

"So far, it's been nothing."

"Not true."

"You haven't even touched me."

"But you've touched me," he spoke thoughtfully. "In some kind of . . . significant way."

"Significant?" She couldn't comprehend his meaning.

"You've given me some . . . stability." He emphasized the last word.

"That's a fucking laugh," she scowled. "Me giving anyone . . . stability."

"Laugh all you want, Christina. But I'm trying to change my life. And you're helping me do it"

She didn't know what to say. She could see that he was serious. Yet the idea of her changing anyone's life fit right into the same category as her giving anyone stability. She couldn't remember ever changing anyone's life—at least not in any significant way, to use his term—except maybe for the worse.

"Want to play?" he pointed to the Scrabble game.

"I'd like to play," she affirmed. "But not Scrabble."

He looked puzzled, which was just fine with her. She could've put six of her letters on the board and made "zebras," connecting the "s" to his "veil" for 45 points. But instead, she grabbed all seven of her letters and flung them onto the floor. She reached for his letters, too, and scattered them all over the room as well.

His only response was an open-mouthed stare. She next took the bag of letters and emptied them onto the floor, too. The Scrabble board and her pipe followed although she handled them more carefully.

Then she focused on him. She shoved him backward, and he nearly tumbled off the bed. Taking advantage of his surprise, she scrambled on top of him and pulled his shirt up, covering his face with it.

"What're you doing?" he stammered.

"What do you think I'm doing?" she answered, her tone high-pitched.

His shirt, an orange long-sleeve knit, was stuck around his face and head. He tried to get free of it but couldn't. He made some kind of guttural sound which she couldn't interpret. She kissed him firmly on the lips, right through the material of his shirt. Seeing his bare chest for the first time emboldened her because she eagerly loosened his belt and tugged at his pants. He tried to slide out from under her, but she wouldn't let him. Only when she heard something rip did she stop tugging.

"What are you doing?" he repeated, his voice sounding frustrated, likely at his shirt still being caught around his head.

"Isn't it obvious?"

"This isn't what I want."

"You said we can do whatever I say. If I agree to your proposal."

"Right."

"I agree to your proposal," she quickly replied.

"You're just saying that," he challenged, finally managing to pull his shirt up over his head.

"Want me to sign a contract?"

"You really mean it?"

"I do. All you have to do is . . . stake your claim."

"Stake my claim?"

"I think," she giggled, "you know what I mean."

He stopped resisting. She was finally able to get his pants off. Still on top of him, she proceeded to take off the rest of his clothes, tossing them individually onto the floor, in a pile. Touching the hair on his chest, she sighed at the sight of his nakedness. Momentarily she felt uneasy because his body, at least compared to hers, appeared so perfect—long, full yet lean, and muscular. Over the years, she'd seen hundreds of male bodies, but she'd always avoided looking closely at them. This was different—she found herself wanting to gaze at every inch of him.

She finally got off him. After taking a deep breath for courage, she quickly took off her grayish-blue blouse and skirt plus the rest of her clothes, placing them all next to his on the floor. Getting back on top of him, she kissed him passionately again, this time without the shirt between them. They traded positions, he getting on top. He kissed her cheek, neck, shoulder, arm. Then he edged sideways, off her.

"I didn't bring a condom," he whispered.

"I have one. But we're not using it."

"That's crazy," he answered sternly. "Why risk some disease?"

"Coward."

"It's more for you than for me. I'm too old to worry."

"I'm not playing safe." She jutted out her chin. "You're the one said . . . it's all or nothing."

"Yeah, but why play roulette?"

"I'm not scared if you're not scared," she said, sticking her tongue out at him.

⋄⟨⊙⟩⋄

Christina's breasts were very small. In fact, her entire chest resembled a little boy's. Pretty much, the only thing clearly feminine about it was her big nipples. Which Daniel kissed and caressed much longer than he needed to. The same had been true for a soft place along her neck.

Her repetitive sighs and moans told him he was pleasing her. Someone else might have proceeded much quicker, but he was in no hurry. He wanted to savor her and these moments because being with her like this incited much stronger feelings in him than he'd ever experienced before.

Although the music from her tape player had stopped much earlier, he hadn't noticed. She apparently did, because she glanced at it on the floor. Or maybe she was trying to locate her pipe, which was in the same general direction. Also, she might have needed a brief interlude from their lovemaking. Whatever the reason for her change in focus, she soon came back to him by reaching up, hugging him, and kissing him ardently again.

"So nice," she whispered in his ear once they parted lips. "So very nice."

He said nothing or did nothing except kiss her again. The thought crossed his mind that she might become impatient, preferring to return to her pipe. Or play some more music. But he'd postponed being with her this way for so long that, if she was willing, he'd want it to last. All night even.

"Why did you make me wait all this time?" she uttered breathlessly, suggesting that, besides her other talents, she might possess some telepathic skills.

He merely shrugged. Then he went back to touching her. More of her sighs informed him when he located additional tactile areas. Her shoulders. The sides of her face just below her ears. The insides of her thighs.

Once more, he sensed that she would rather he speed up, yet he remained steadfast. How could another hour or two compare to all the months it had taken for this to finally happen?

❧❦❧

Christina was glad she had insisted that Daniel not use a condom. This way, she could feel him—the real him, not some rubber-coated version—inside of her. She briefly thought about all the other men she'd had over the years. It was like—because she required that all of them use condoms—they didn't count. They didn't matter. What really mattered was how nice his manhood felt squirming warmly around in her.

"I can't believe how good you feel," she heard herself speak in a voice so sultry she hardly recognized it as her own.

"You're giving me back my life," he whispered in her ear while nibbling on it.

As if to accentuate his comment, he thrust deeply inside her. She stifled a wince because the sincerity she recognized in his statement neutralized any discomfort she felt. Fortunately, he returned to his slow, methodical style, with movements barely discernible. She couldn't help thinking that, despite all her complaints and criticism to the contrary, what she admired most in him was his deliberateness, his overriding patience.

"Had enough?" he asked, again nibbling at her ear.

"No, no," she sighed.

"Just checking."

With a sudden quick movement, he threatened another deep thrust. She anticipated some pain, but it never occurred. Instead of surging again, he kissed her passionately once more and pressed ever so slightly deeper inside her.

⚬

"Well, I finally beat you," Daniel announced.

"At what?" Christina asked, acting puzzled, although she had a pretty good idea.

"At Scrabble, *silly*," he taunted.

Of course, she recognized that he had just referred to her in the same way she often referred to him. He was lying beside her in bed, leaning on his left elbow. Their clothes were still on the floor.

"You didn't beat me," she said, rising in protest while keeping herself covered with the bedsheet.

"Sure, I did," he laughed, nodding at the scorecard nearby. "Fourteen-nothing."

"We didn't finish the game."

"Oh? You want to keep playing?"

"We can't," she countered irritably, eyeing some of the letters on the floor.

"Well, then, I won. Fourteen-nothing."

"We didn't finish the game," she repeated sternly.

"I guess you didn't like your letters," he smirked. "Why else toss them all over the place?"

"You know very well why I tossed them all over the place."

He laughed again. She nearly laughed herself, but she wasn't about to give him the satisfaction. In truth, her irritability, which she deliberately persisted with, was feigned because she felt so good. After all her concerns about her body, their lovemaking had been wonderful. No question he cared for her. And this had been the first time in many years that she'd actually "made love" to a man.

"Oh, did I adequately," he winked, "stake my claim?"

"Very adequately." She couldn't keep from giggling once more.

"I'll give you a rematch," he offered, smiling.

"In Scrabble? Or in . . . staking your claim?"

"In Scrabble, *silly*?"

"It wouldn't be a rematch," she debated. "But I'll tell you what. We'll pick up the letters and start over. And I'll give you your crummy fourteen points. As a head start."

"Big deal," he complained. "Instead of like 260 points, you'll only beat me by say . . . 246."

"I plan to beat you by a shitload more than that." She stuck her tongue out at him again.

PART II

Chapter Ten

My heart was doing its usual thump-thump-thumping as I began dialing. It was probably worse this time because when I'd dialed the number I had for Dad, a recording came on, which said that that number was disconnected. I first thought that now there'd be no way to reach him and that he'd left the San Francisco area, so that my call would serve no purpose. But luckily, the recording gave a new number, which at least did have a San Francisco area code. Someone picked up the receiver on the other end, and I held my breath.

"Hello."

"Have you moved, Dad?" I blurted out in my excitement at the sound of his voice.

"Tara, is that you?"

"Yes, Dad, it's me."

"Yes, I've moved. To a place not too far from my old one."

I was relieved. Not that my heart wasn't still thumping away. Like during our other conversation, I was sitting on my bed.

"Dad, I have some good news." I tried to sound cheerful, hoping he would share my optimism.

"I'm glad, honey. Tell me."

"Mother said I could pick a college in your area."

That's wonderful, honey." He sounded genuinely pleased.

"But I also have some bad news."

"What is it, Tara? Are you okay?"

"I'm fine. But I'm afraid my grades aren't. They're nowhere near good enough to get into a good college there."

"You've got plenty of time to bring them up, honey."

His encouragement helped. So did his soothing tone. He was right; I did have time. I still had three full years.

"How's your mother and sister?" he asked.

"Both fine. How are you, Dad?"

"I'm fine, too."

There was a pause, which seemed a little strained. Like the other time, I looked up at the painting of the ocean above my bed. Like then, it offered no help in what to say next. I could hear Mother and Stacy chatting in our living room and hoped they hadn't heard me talking.

"Tara, don't worry about anything." His voice sounded soothing again. "Things are going to be okay."

"Thanks, Dad."

We said good-bye. After we hung up, I remained on my bed and wondered when I'd see him next. Whether I'd have to wait until college. Or if I'd even see him then.

⋅⟨◉⟩⋅

During the first week or so after they moved into their new apartment, Daniel had never seen Christina so consistently happy. She had a perpetual smile on her face. Despite her clear love of music, he'd never heard her do any singing. Not until that week anyway, when he discovered what a nice melodic voice she possessed. And she couldn't keep from regularly praising the attributes of their new residence.

It was she who'd selected it, furnished and in a blue-collar suburb five or six miles from downtown San Francisco. Although agonizing over moving from her old neighborhood, with its familiarity and permissiveness, she repeatedly emphasized that this new phase of their relationship merited a fresh locale. He remained neutral in this entire process, which culminated in trips to Grandma's flat and his old apartment to retrieve their belongings.

She'd already led him on a couple of walks to the quaint little business district known as Glen Park, less than half a mile away. It was nestled in a valley with ascending sidewalks leading up into heavily populated hills. The commercial area was old and had a distinct "small town" flavor. He'd commented that its architecture, shops, and restaurants evoked a mood of the 1940s and 50s. She was thrilled that there was a branch, albeit tiny, of the public library, and a subway station offering a mere ten-minute ride to downtown.

"I love our backyard," she'd enthused on their very first day there, leading him from the apartment into a white-fenced grassy space with abundant trees, plants, and flowers.

"You don't think the apartment's too small?" he'd asked, nodding toward it from the yard.

"Hardly," she refuted. "It's a mansion compared to what I'm used to."

"Okay," he shrugged.

But he was right—the place was small. It had only a little bedroom, a minimal kitchen, and a tiny bathroom. What sparse furniture there was was old and a little shopworn.

"The rent's low," she said appeasingly and almost apologetically.

"We can afford more."

"One problem, though," she cautioned.

"What?"

"Big change from the old neighborhood. We're kinda remote out here."

"Remote?" He was puzzled because her comment didn't fit with the local population density.

"Well," she frowned and spoke softly in case anyone else was within earshot. "Not exactly a . . . dealer on every corner."

"Good," he quickly replied.

"Not so good," she said, shaking her head. "Low supply, high price."

He didn't respond, other than to grit his teeth, reminding them both that this wasn't his favorite topic.

"I could always take the subway into the old neighborhood," she offered softly. "To keep costs down."

"Don't bother," he grumbled.

⟡

Daniel continued to do well with the sports tour company, developing several new clients in the San Francisco area. One night about three weeks after he and Christina had moved to the new place, he got in from work much later than usual, a little after dark. Christina wasn't home yet, not unusual for her lately.

He'd noticed that her initial contentment with the apartment had waned somewhat. Her frequent smile had become sporadic, and her singing had pretty much ceased. He certainly didn't like it—her doing whatever she did after dark. But he had to acknowledge that she had her own life, especially while he was away at work, and needed plenty of freedom. No way could he keep her under lock and key.

He'd had a long day—calling on several prospective clients, both in-person and by phone—and he was tired. His business clothes still on, he went into the bedroom and laid down. He dozed off right away. And dreamed. He and Christina were playing Scrabble and, nearing the end of the game—something that could happen only in a dream—he was indeed ahead.

"Wake up, lazy."

Christina's greeting startled him out of his sleep. It also miffed him a little because it short-circuited his making 89 points. He was about to bingo on a triple word score with "stirrups," which would have widened his lead to more than a hundred. No way could he lose. Fair and square, without a "head start."

He sat up in bed groggily. He could tell she'd turned on a light in the kitchen, since it shined in his eyes. She was standing over him, wearing a brown pantsuit he'd never seen before.

"What time is it?" he asked.

"Ten-thirty."

"That late?"

"Not too late to play Scrabble," she answered.

San Francisco Story | **109**

Were he not groggy, he might've pointed out that they were about to finish a game, and he was walloping her. Instead, he simply watched her turn on a bedroom light and take the Scrabble board out of its box. Because she looked so serious, he suspected that she was trying to hide something, and he decided to probe.

"Can I ask where you were?"

"You know." She raised her eyebrows.

"Scoring?"

"Right."

"So late?"

"Dealer wasn't there when he was supposed to be."

"Guy around here?" he asked.

"No. Downtown. Might try someone else soon. Except his stuff's always so good." She took a small gray tin from her backpack and put it on the night table.

"Maybe try someone around here," he suggested.

"Maybe."

⊰⊱

Straight ahead, as she walked in her old neighborhood, Christina spotted Uncle Harold. She didn't know what to do. Whether to turn around and dash the other way, hoping he didn't see her. Or, since it was dusk, with daylight diminishing, try to slip by on the sidewalk, which was sprinkled with other pedestrians. Too late—he saw her and approached.

"Hi, Christina," he greeted enthusiastically. "Out and about?"

"Hello, Uncle Harold."

"Looking for business?" he asked a bit accusingly, almost under his breath.

"No, no, nothing like that," she answered defensively. "Just wandering."

It was true. At least once a week, she took the Bart into downtown and visited her old haunts. No question, she missed seeing the familiar faces and places. Grandma, thrift shops, the old pink "Humpty Dumpty" wall among them. This evening she was headed for the downtown public library, hoping to find a book the Glen Park branch didn't have.

Not that she hadn't been getting along decently enough with Daniel during their first month or so of living together. It was just that the little apartment was so confining, with constant proximity to each other. Plus, she didn't exactly trust her ability to sustain a relationship. And if things did fall apart, she'd better have a backup plan.

"Good to see you," Uncle Harold said, touching her hand.

"Good to see you, too."

Again, she was speaking the truth. Even in the failing light, she could make out the sparkle in his blue eyes, probably his best feature. Like the other people and places from the old neighborhood, she missed him. And not only for his generosity. No, she especially liked his patience and understanding. How, for example, when she'd called him to let him know she had to stop seeing him—after she'd agreed to Daniel's proposal—he told her that his door would always be open and he even wished her luck.

"I haven't found someone else yet," he admitted.

"I'm sorry."

"Things working out for you?"

"So far," she shrugged.

He didn't reply right away. His eager expression suggested he was about to invite her to his apartment right then. His art museum of a living room flashed through her mind. As good as he'd been to her, she hated the prospect of turning him down. But she knew that's what she'd do. So, she was very relieved when the frown on his face indicated he'd changed his mind about asking.

"Let me know," he said, "if your situation changes."

"Okay," she promised.

And then, practically in the next heartbeat, he was gone. She began walking again toward the library.

⚬⟨⊙⟩⚬

"I have a friend in the bedroom," Christina welcomed as Daniel, briefcase in hand, entered their apartment after getting in from work.

"I don't feel like seeing anyone," he replied irritably.

"But I want you to meet them."

"I'm a little tired."

"Come on. Just say hello."

He held his ground near the front door. This couldn't be good. Likely a former lover or drug dealer from her old neighborhood. Surely not someone he'd care to make small talk with. She took his arm, though, and practically dragged him away from the door. Warily, he followed her into the bedroom.

"Daniel, meet Dark Star," she announced with mock formality. "Dark Star, meet Daniel."

He couldn't help breaking out laughing. Sitting on the floor, wagging its tail, was a small black and white dog. It slinked meekly to them. Christina bent over and patted its head. Although the dog looked primarily like a cocker spaniel, Daniel assumed it to be a mix.

"Where did you get her?" he asked, still laughing.

"Him," she quickly corrected.

"Him. Where did you get *him*?"

"The old neighborhood. His owner got sent up."

"You're not thinking of keeping him?"

"Only if you don't mind another mouth to feed."

He didn't respond right away. The dog tried to lick Daniel's ankle under his pant leg. Reluctantly Daniel reached down and scratched him behind an ear.

"Is Dark Star his real name?" he asked.

"No. I gave it to him. When I was a kid, we had a dog that looked like him. My father named him after some racehorse he liked."

The dog tried licking Daniel's ankle again. Once more, Daniel reluctantly scratched him, switching to behind the other ear. He could feel himself begin to smile, but he forced himself not to.

"Dark Star won a Kentucky Derby," he declared as if about to win big money on a quiz show. "In one of the most famous upsets in horse racing history."

Christina smiled. This time, instead of trying to lick Daniel, Dark Star wagged his tail at him.

⚜

An unexpected benefit of Daniel assenting to Dark Star joining the household was that Christina was almost always home when he got in from work. So, it felt strange that she wasn't there one evening when he didn't get back until nearly nine o'clock. He'd been making a presentation to a trial attorney association taking a tour to L.A. for a baseball series between the Giants and the Dodgers.

He immediately checked the apartment for any possible clue to where she might be this late. She could've left a note or a phone message. There might've been some sign of a visitor—a cigarette butt in an ashtray or a half-empty beer can. Were there clothes askew on the bed, it could've suggested a hasty departure. But he found nothing, not the slightest trace of anything revealing.

He sat down in the only chair in the bedroom, a La-Z-Boy with several adjustable positions. He was tired enough to doze off, but he didn't dare because he feared she was in some kind of trouble. His focus alternated mostly between the phone and the front door.

Dark Star jumped up into his lap. He had settled in nicely during his two weeks as a family member. Daniel might've taken him for a walk, except he was so intent on Christina`s whereabouts that he decided to wait.

The phone rang. He leaped up off the La-Z-Boy, nearly tipping it over while sending Dark Star tumbling rudely to the floor. The instant he said hello, he could tell Christina was on the other end by the rapid way she was breathing.

"Not coming home tonight," she spoke solemnly.

"Why not?"

"Jail."

"Jail?"

"That's where I am. I'm in jail."

"What for!" he exclaimed, alarmed.

"For being fucking stupid."

"Drugs?"

"Brilliant."

Not good news, but at least it was news, and he no longer had to wonder where she was. He glanced at Dark Star and motioned him over, but he was obviously angry at being dumped to the floor and wasn't about to come. Instead, he jumped back up on the La-Z-Boy, seemingly happy to have it entirely to himself.

"I'll come get you," Daniel told Christina.

"No, no," she put him off. "They haven't started processing me yet. And prob'ly won't fucking get around to it for a while."

"I'll wait with you."

"They won't let you. Come in the morning."

"This is crazy." He could feel his pulse rate rising. "I don't want you spending the night in jail."

"Don't worry. It's only a holding cell."

Of course, the mere mention of jail and a holding cell only added to his distress, as he flashed back to his own night of incarceration in L.A. But what could he do—sit in some awful waiting room all night? Did they even have a waiting room? For some reason, he looked at his hand that wasn't holding the phone and saw it was shaking.

"Daniel . . ." Her voice was subdued.

"Yes."

"Be sure to feed Dark Star before you go to bed. And walk him."

"Right," he answered less than cheerfully while glancing again at the dog, sprawled out comfortably on the La-Z-Boy.

⟡

"You going to tell me what happened?" Daniel asked as he and Christina walked from the jail to his car the next morning, following her release.

"Fell into their fucking trap."

"Whose?"

"Undercover."

"Where?" he continued the inquiry.

"The old neighborhood."

He shook his head. Definitely not for the first time that morning. The jail waiting room, where he'd just spent a couple of hours, had smelled rancid. The crowd there to visit inmates fit the seedy décor. But his biggest head-shaker was the recollection of all his sordid activities leading eventually to his own incarceration that dreadful night in L.A., and the single prevailing question—how could he have done what he did?

At least there had been some good news of sorts. In the jail waiting room, he'd spotted the burly guy from that first miserable hotel in San Francisco, the one where the woman in black had handcuffed him to the bed. Daniel approached the guy and thanked him for rescuing him, and finally had the opportunity to give him that long-delayed reward money he'd promised.

The morning was gray and overcast, not unusual for San Francisco in July, a weather pattern he'd grown accustomed to. To make the time to pick her up, he'd already canceled a couple of business appointments for the day and anticipated more changes, which he wasn't happy about. As they continued toward his car, she stared straight ahead and didn't look especially happy herself. At a red light, they stopped on the sidewalk.

"So, what happens next?" he asked.

"When the light changes, we fucking cross the street."

"You know what I mean."

"I go to a hearing," she muttered barely above a whisper. "Where they offer some kind of bullshit plea bargain."

He nodded. She kept on staring straight ahead. The light changed, and they did cross the street. A passing car honked. Although she didn't acknowledge the driver, she eyed him briefly, as if she knew him.

"Someone make bail for you?" he queried a bit suspiciously.

"Yes. A friend."

"What friend?"

"What difference does it make?"

"You sure there wasn't something else to this?" he probed further.

"Like what?"

"Like something else."

"You mean like," she said while finally glancing at him, although her hostility remained, "was I fucking looking for a customer?"

His shrug conveyed an affirmative answer.

"I gave you my word," she spit out.

This time he frowned, expressing his doubt.

"You don't believe me," she declared even more angrily, "we can damn well walk right back to the jail and read the fucking police report."

"I believe you," he quickly replied, despite not being sure he did. He'd spent more than enough time around a jail for one morning.

Chapter Eleven

"I hope you like spaghetti, Alfredo," Christina said while placing a big platter of it on the kitchen table. "I make it all the time."

"Yes, I do, Mrs. Coach."

Robert Lawson smiled at Alfredo's reference to Christina. Daniel smiled too. His reaction, though, was more from the fact that the only three people he was close to in San Francisco were here, about to have dinner with him.

He glanced at each of them. First at Alfredo--Hispanic, growing up in this country as an orphan. Then at Lawson, a black man with only one arm. Finally, at Christina, a recent escapee from the streets. And he, Daniel, certainly fit right in, being estranged from his family and exiled in San Francisco.

"Where's Dark Star?" Christina asked while filling his water bowl. "He's never far from food."

That reminded Daniel that Dark Star, with his former owner in prison, also fit this diversity. Daniel went into the bedroom to look for him. No sign. The bathroom—same result. Then he noticed the front door slightly ajar. And remembered that he might have left it open after getting a new Giants cap from his Buick for Alfredo.

"I think I'm to blame," he anxiously admitted after returning to the kitchen. "Looks like he's gotten out."

Christina glared at him. Clearly distraught, she rushed to the front door and went outside. She didn't even stop to take off the white apron she was wearing. Daniel followed. So did Lawson and Alfredo. Daniel caught up to her on the sidewalk in front of the apartment.

"Let's split up," she instructed while glaring at him again. "Everyone go a different direction."

She went on, heading south. When the other two reached Daniel, he pointed Lawson east and Alfredo north. He started west. Fortunately, night hadn't fallen yet. But it was dusk, with not much light remaining.

As he walked, he felt awful. While calling out Dark Star's name, he could hear the anguish in his own voice. In addition to being to blame, he'd grown fond of the dog.

Up ahead, he heard barking. It sounded like Dark Star. He sped up hopefully. However, when he got close, he saw it was a border collie in a fenced yard, yapping at a hissing cat.

After trekking a couple of blocks, he doubled back on another street. He kept calling out Dark Star's name, with no response. He was becoming more disheartened. Maybe the others had had luck. He decided to check back.

Nearing the apartment in the twilight, he could barely spot Alfredo kneeling on the sidewalk. With something beside him. Maybe a black and white dog? Yes, it was Dark Star. Daniel felt a rush of joy as he approached them.

Lawson arrived then, too. So did Christina, still wearing the white apron. She first threw her arms around Dark Star, who was panting from his excursion and then around Alfredo, who had ahold of the collar around the dog's neck.

"He okay?" she asked Alfredo.

"He is fine, Mrs. Coach."

"Where was he?"

"Near a pizza parlor, Mrs. Coach. He was looking inside."

"I guess," Daniel cracked to Christina, "he likes pizza better than your spaghetti."

She glared at him once more.

"Daniel, I'm letting you off the hook," Christina said, her tone somber.

"Letting me off the hook?" he replied. "For what?"

"For all the mouths you're feeding."

"Big deal. You, me and Dark Star."

While looking straight ahead, she paused, apparently seeking just the right words. It was a warm early-August day, and the two of them were outside near the apartment, walking Dark Star. When she spoke again, her voice was equally somber.

"Something you don't know . . ."

"What don't I know?"

"There's another mouth."

"Another dog?" he guessed.

"Not another dog."

"What, then?"

"Well . . ."

"Well, what?"

"Well," she said, turning toward him. "I'm pregnant."

"Pregnant . . ." The word slipped almost involuntarily from his lips.

Neither of them spoke again right away. She was undoubtedly waiting for his reaction, and he was a little stunned by the news. Dark Star stopped to sniff some grass. Christina pulled on his leash, but he resisted moving on, so she waited.

"Are you sure?" Daniel finally asked.

"Two-and-a-half months sure. I went to a clinic the other day."

"Why didn't you say something sooner?"

"I had to think about it."

"I see."

Really, he didn't see, but he was still a bit too shocked to be very expressive. Dark Star decided to head on, so they all did. He growled at a cat and tried to chase it. Christina held the leash firm, thwarting him.

"So," she said, "this lets you off the hook."

"Is that what you want? Me off the hook."

"What I want is to be fair. You agreed to my expenses. No one said anything about a dog. *And* a baby."

"You mean you're going to keep it?" he asked, surprised.

"Yes."

"You're sure?"

"I'm sure," she sounded definite.

"Christina, I need to ask you something." He was feeling more lucid.

"What?"

"The baby. Is it mine?"

"Yes."

"How do you know? I mean, I'm probably too old to get you pregnant."

"Simple," she answered straightforwardly. "You and me, we never use a rubber. With everyone else, I always insisted."

Dark Star eyed some birds flying overhead. He crouched like he wanted to chase them, or even fly alongside. Daniel glanced at Christina, who, for some reason, looked content.

"I think we'll need a bigger place," he said.

⋅⟨◉⟩⋅

Most kids want to go to movies or play videos when they go out with their "big brothers." Not Alfredo. He wanted to go to a dog shelter. Truth was, ever since he rescued Dark Star near the pizza parlor, visiting a dog shelter had been his constant request of Daniel. Which was exactly where they were now, on a sunny late-August Saturday afternoon.

"I like dogs, Coach," was Alfredo's simple explanation.

When they arrived at the shelter—an old gray edifice not far from Alfredo's foster home—they were met by a pony-tailed male attendant in his twenties. He guided them through the building where fifty or so canines were housed. Daniel was dismayed by the incessant barking and whimpering of the caged dogs. When Alfredo spotted a black and white shivering at the back of its cage, he asked the attendant if he could walk it. The attendant entered the cage, leashed the dog, and handed the leash to Alfredo.

"This dog looks like Dark Star," the boy clarified after he led it outside, onto a grassy fenced area adjacent to the building.

Indeed, the dog did resemble Dark Star. Besides being black and white, it was at least partly cocker spaniel like Dark Star. And it even sounded like Dark Star when it barked at another dog nearby.

"How long has he been here?" Daniel asked the attendant while nodding toward the dog, who'd stopped shivering by then.

"She."

"She," Daniel laughed, recalling the gender error he'd made when Christina introduced him to Dark Star.

"She's been here about a week," the young man answered Daniel's question.

"How long before . . . ?" Daniel began a new, disturbing question.

"We're a no-kill shelter," the guy interrupted. "No time limit."

"What is her name?" Alfredo interjected.

"Lucky."

"Can I come back and walk her again?"

"Sure. If she hasn't been adopted."

"Can I come back and walk some of the other dogs, too?"

"Sure. All day long."

Alfredo smiled in response.

"In fact," the attendant continued, "maybe you'd like to volunteer here. We can use some help."

"I'm sure he'd like to adopt a dog," Daniel ventured, feeling a little funny because he knew that adoption was the main purpose of the shelter. "But I don't think they'll let him have one where he lives now."

"Why do I want only one dog, Coach?" Alfredo questioned. "When maybe I can take care of many dogs here."

The attendant grinned. Then he excused himself when other people came into the grassy area. Alfredo kneeled and rubbed Lucky's neck and shoulders. She purred as if she were a cat or had often been around cats. Daniel would have suggested they walk another dog or two, but he and Alfredo were to meet Lawson and one of his "little brothers" soon. Besides, he had another type of adoption to bring up.

"Ever think about a family, Alfredo?"

"Not much, Coach." His expression was blank.

"A mother and a father? Maybe a little brother or sister?"

"Not much, Coach." He continued to show no enthusiasm. "I think I am too old."

Daniel recognized that Alfredo's lack of response was likely caused by his being passed over for adoption many times before. No question, prospective parents preferred babies or much younger children. The boy got up from his kneeling position and began to walk Lucky again.

"Coach Lawson knows some adoption people," Daniel said from alongside. "He thinks maybe Christina and I could become your family. And she's soon to have a little brother or sister. Plus, let's not forget Dark Star."

"That would be nice, Coach." Alfredo showed a bit more enthusiasm.

"And you wouldn't have to call me Coach anymore. You could call me Dad or Father or Papa."

"I will call you whatever you want," he replied sincerely. "Just so you will still be my coach."

It was time for them to leave. They walked Lucky back into the old gray edifice and turned her over to the attendant. Once more, Daniel felt dismayed by all the barking and whimpering from the caged dogs.

⋅◈⋅

"Am I imagining things?" Daniel asked Christina. "Or have you been smoking your pipe less lately?"

"Very observant."

"Because of the baby?"

She shrugged. They were sitting at a table in an elegant nightclub atop a luxurious hotel, a spectacular view of San Francisco spreading out before them. Crystal chandeliers hung from the high ceiling, and a polished wooden dance floor was close by. They'd already been there nearly three hours, had dinner, and danced to several songs performed by an upbeat swing band, now on break. Predictably, like with their Scrabble competition, she was a much better dancer than he. She was limited only by her condition, beginning to show, and its effect on her stamina.

"Do me a favor," he said.

"What?" she replied without much enthusiasm.

"Go into the restroom."

"And?"

"And," he whispered carefully while deliberately smiling mischievously, "take off your panties."

"What on earth do you want me to take off my panties for?" she whispered back.

"For me."

"For you? But I've taken my panties off for you only about a zillion times."

"Not here." He was still smiling.

"You mean not in public." She smoothed the lovely red dress he'd bought her for the occasion.

"I guess so if you want to make that distinction."

She paused, obviously considering. He noticed a wrinkle in the navy-blue suit he had on, her favorite in his limited wardrobe. The band members began returning to the stage at the front of the club, and he anticipated that if they started playing, she'd avoid his proposal by suggesting they dance. Laughter from some of the patrons broke out nearby—to his left, her right—and they both glanced in their direction.

"One condition," she presented what he by now recognized as her trademark way of giving in.

"What?"

"That we stop for ice cream on the way home. I'm having cravings."

"Chocolate or vanilla?" he grinned.

"Jamocha almond fudge. I even dream of it."

"Like I dream of a pretty girl in a red dress. Wearing no panties."

She giggled. She got up and headed toward the restroom. The band began playing again. He listened—it was an upbeat Ray Charles song, "I Got a Woman." At first, he kept the beat by tapping his fingers on the table and his feet on the floor. Then he mouthed the words, "I got a woman, clear cross town. She's good to me. Oh, yeah." When Christina returned, he was still mouthing and tapping.

"You're sure in a good mood," she said dryly.

"Why shouldn't I be?"

"I did it."

"Where are they?" he asked, still tapping his fingers on the table.

"In my purse. Wanna see?"

"Sure."

Deliberately smiling mischievously again, he leaned over and looked under the table. Naturally, she realized he was about to look up her dress, so she reached out and pushed him upright.

"No, silly," she laughed. "In my purse."

"I believe you," he laughed too.

The band finished the number. They began another Ray Charles song—a slow one, "Georgia on My Mind." Although the lead singer, a male, was slightly off tune, it sounded good. This time Daniel started humming in accompaniment.

"Don't forget about my jamocha almond fudge," Christina interrupted.

"I won't. Want to dance?"

"It's slow."

"I know. I promise not to dip you."

"So, what if you do?" she said.

"Someone might see something." He purposely sounded lascivious.

"Who cares about seeing a pregnant woman without panties?" she asked flatly.

"I do," he answered promptly while getting up to lead her to the dance floor.

Chapter Twelve

Finally, three full months after Christina's arrest and night in jail, the date for her pre-trial hearing arrived. It had been postponed twice. The first time was because a brief janitorial strike forced the temporary closure of the courthouse, located near downtown San Francisco. A backlog of cases caused the second one, with more important cases taking precedent over hers.

Daniel felt tense as he sat down at a table in a small, drab, very stuffy side room at the courthouse. He glanced at Christina, sitting beside him, and her facial expression registered tension also. They had joined a tall, lanky male district attorney representative and a balding, fiftyish court-appointed referee, both seated across the table from them.

"Mr. Stanton," the referee began by addressing Daniel, "since you're here, may I ask your official relationship to the defendant?"

"We live together." Daniel could hear the strain in his own voice.

"As husband and wife?"

"No."

"So, you're very aware of her drug use."

"Lately, I haven't seen her use at all." Daniel forced himself to sound resolute.

"She's stopped completely?"

"I haven't seen her use at all," Daniel repeated.

"What are your plans with her?"

"Well," Daniel said, looking at Christina, "I hope to . . . marry her. If she'd have me."

The referee nodded. He sifted through some papers. Then he turned to the DA rep.

"I think you have to admit that your case isn't as tight as you'd like."

The DA rep fidgeted. A ray of hope replaced some of Daniel's tension. Even though it was still early morning, the room was very warm, and he'd started sweating.

"For your information," the referee said, glancing first at Christina and then at Daniel, "undercover officers almost always tape-record their actions. In this instance, their tape wasn't decipherable."

"Both officers are willing to testify," the DA rep debated.

"Still becomes their word against hers."

The DA rep fidgeted some more. Daniel began to feel even more optimistic. He looked at Christina again, for some indication of her disposition. She displayed none.

"Miss Lambeau," the referee continued, facing Christina, "at the risk of sounding personal, may I ask when your baby is due?"

"Late January or early February, sir. In a little more than three months."

"You realize that with your prison record, conviction might mean at least a two-year sentence."

Daniel grimaced and clenched and unclenched his fists. Christina sighed. Daniel observed that an overhead light was reflecting off the referee's bald head.

"The DA's case is thin, though," the referee went on after brief hesitation, "and our prisons are already overcrowded. Plus, it appears that the defendant is making good progress in her life. So, I'm prepared to offer you a concession, Miss Lambeau. I'm prepared to recommend only two months in county jail."

Daniel noticed that the DA rep's expression was blank. Christina looked a little relieved. He was more puzzled than anything.

"Would you give us some time to discuss this?" he asked the referee.

"Certainly. Why don't you step outside?"

Daniel nodded. He took Christina's hand and led her out of the room. The corridor outside was no less drab and stuffy, but at least it wasn't as warm. He guided her to a little alcove with a window offering a view of the street three floors below. He could feel anger welling up inside him.

"I guess that's what you meant by a bullshit plea bargain," he said, recalling her statement of months earlier.

"It's not as bullshit as I thought it would be." She was much calmer than he was.

"I don't like it one bit! You pregnant and in jail. I think we should fight. Go to trial if we have to. You heard him say their case is thin."

She frowned. A man and a woman walked by, the woman holding a baby. Christina appeared deep in thought as she watched them go down the hall.

"You're forgetting something," she said, turning back to Daniel.

"What am I forgetting?"

"We go to trial and lose," she spoke firmly, "the baby might be born in jail. Or worse, I'm in jail after the baby's born."

He didn't reply. He realized that there was nothing more to say.

⁕

The initial days of Christina's incarceration were difficult for Daniel. To try to keep his mind off the fact that she was pregnant, stuck in jail, and that he missed her badly, he busied himself as best he could. Things like going to work very early in the morning. Taking Dark Star for long walks. Frequent outings with Alfredo, including going to dog shelters with him.

Christina had promised to phone him each evening at seven, and he looked forward to that every day. One night about a week and a half into her confinement, the phone rang a few minutes before seven. He was just getting in from work and nearly tripped over Dark Star while hurrying to answer it.

"When can I come visit?" he blurted out a greeting.

"Be patient," Christina urged.

"But I want to see you."

"You won't like what you see."

Those last words had been her constant excuse for not allowing him to visit. And "be patient" had been her incessant admonition. He'd tried several ways to convince her otherwise—from she'd seen *him* at his worst at least a hundred times, to he was sure she looked better than all the other inmates combined—but she remained steadfast. He'd just have to keep himself busy until she was ready.

"How's Dark Star?" she asked.

"Getting plenty of exercise."

"Good."

"He misses you."

"I miss him."

"The baby okay?"

"No problems. The prison nurse said I'm doing fine."

"I miss you too," he said.

"And I, you," she replied, barely above a whisper. "Be patient."

"What choice do I have? Unless I make a reverse jailbreak."

"Reverse jailbreak?"

"Most people want to break out of jail," he laughed at what he really didn't find funny. "I want to break in."

"Be patient," she said once more, obviously not finding it funny either.

❧◦❧

Visiting day finally arrived. It came on Thanksgiving, and Christina relented because, according to her, that day merited human companionship. Sure, she acknowledged that Daniel had Dark Star, but, she explained, a dog was only a dog.

Little did she know that he would have plenty of human companionship on Thanksgiving. He wasn't about to tell her, though, concerned she'd change her mind about his visiting. His Chicago athletic club tour group had come into town for the Bears-49ers football game, and he met them at the airport.

Because of the positive time change for westbound flights, he'd been able to arrange a morning arrival. He hired a motor coach, driver, and

tour guide to provide local sightseeing, and he went along, too. He envisioned that someday, with his great love for San Francisco, he'd be doing
the guiding and narration himself, but for the moment, he'd just have to
be satisfied being a passenger.

After they viewed the city's major attractions—Golden Gate Park
and Twin Peaks included—the motor coach dropped them at the hotel
Daniel reserved. Following check-in, they had lunch. He informed them
that later that afternoon, he might join them for Thanksgiving dinner at
a restaurant he'd selected.

Before that, however, he headed for the jail.

⋅⟨◉⟩⋅

Getting in to see Christina turned out to be no easy proposition.
It took much of the afternoon. When Daniel entered the jail lobby, he
found many visitors there ahead of him, waiting to see prisoners on the
holiday. In addition, visiting hours were interrupted at three o'clock for
Thanksgiving dinner, for jail staff and inmates alike.

Finally, after five-thirty, he and about a dozen other people were ush-
ered up a flight of stairs to the visiting area. By that time, the long wait
had dampened his anticipation at seeing her. The fact that it was taking
place at a jail didn't help. Not only did he continue to be dismayed about
her confinement, but he was nowhere near shaking the memory of his
own night of incarceration in L.A. Before sitting down on his side of
the thick glass that separated visitors from prisoners, he handed a guard
an envelope with six one-dollar bills inside, the maximum amount that
could be left for an inmate to purchase incidentals like toothpaste and
shampoo.

A group of prisoners, all wearing gray uniforms, entered the large
room through a steel door. Daniel looked for Christina and spotted her.
She came over and sat down across from him. Hardly any privacy was
possible since small microphones were positioned to amplify sound on
each side of the thick glass.

"I warned you," were the first words she spoke into her mike.

Indeed, she had. And for good reason. He hardly recognized her. Her eyes were puffy, with deep circles underneath. She looked pale and thinner than usual, her pregnancy making the latter all the more apparent. Her long dark hair, normally one of her best features, lacked vibrancy and color. Although she didn't often use make-up, her lifeless complexion could have benefitted from some.

During a couple of their seven o'clock phone conversations, they'd discussed the fact that she had abstained from drugs since her jail term began. And that withdrawal had never been easy. No doubt that was a significant contributor to her appearance. Still, despite all this, he was thrilled to see her.

"You look beautiful to me," he spoke somewhat less than truthfully.

"Your eyesight is bad," she replied.

He shrugged. She smiled at him. He could tell she was happy to see him too.

"Daniel . . ."

"Yes?"

"Were you serious . . . about what you said at the hearing?"

"Of course." He vaguely recalled his statement to the referee about her drug use. "I hadn't seen you smoke lately."

"Not about my smoking."

"What, then?"

"About that other thing you said."

"What other thing?"

"About . . . hoping to marry me," she smiled again. "If I'd have you."

"Yes . . . sure," he answered a little hesitantly once he remembered that part of his testimony.

"Well, I'd have you," she quickly said, smiling once more, this time brightly.

He didn't reply because he was a bit stunned. He anxiously glanced around the room for an indication of someone listening, but he didn't see any. Meanwhile, her smile turned into a wide grin.

"What a clever way to propose," she praised.

"I can be clever sometimes," he said reflexively.

"You sure you still want to?"

"When?" was the best he could manage.

"I thought like . . . maybe in a few weeks. Like on Christmas Day."

"Christmas Day?" he stammered, still a little overwhelmed by the whole idea. "Where?"

"Here."

"In jail!" he exclaimed.

"They said it would help morale for the holidays."

"Sounds like you've got it all worked out."

The twinkle in her eyes told him that she did. He looked around the room again for any sign of someone overhearing them, but once more saw none. Then he took a deep breath.

"Don't you think it's appropriate?" she enthused. "Getting engaged on Thanksgiving and married on Christmas."

"Right," he muttered. "And the baby'll probably be born on New Year's."

"Good idea," she grinned again.

He didn't reply right away. Instead, he looked up at a wall clock behind her. It was already a few minutes past six, too late to join the Chicago tour group for dinner. He'd just have to have a little Thanksgiving meal with Dark Star and let all this sink in.

"I better get going," he said, starting to get up.

"So soon," she challenged.

"Is there a penalty for leaving early?" he chuckled.

"No. No penalty."

"I don't go now," he spoke with mock seriousness, "I might not get home in time for your seven o'clock phone call."

She laughed.

Chapter Thirteen

The Chicago Bears *were* undefeated, as Daniel and the athletic club representative had conjectured when they first discussed the tour several months earlier. But their unblemished record was in jeopardy. With four seconds remaining in the game, they trailed the 49ers, 19-17.

The Bears field goal kicker, Stephan Wojokowski, eyed the goal post. He was about to attempt a 42-yarder. If he made the kick, the Bears would win, 20-19.

All afternoon a frigid swirling wind had howled off the bay adjacent to Candlestick Park, the home stadium of the 49ers. Right then, it seemed to blow its hardest, offering 49er fans hope that it would hinder the kick. They hissed and jeered, trying to rattle Wojokowski.

Daniel, sitting high above the fifty-yard line, amid his Chicago tour group, was colder than he'd been all afternoon. And he'd been cold since the opening kickoff. Hoping for a successful kick and a Bears victory, he crossed all his fingers on both hands.

As a strategy to try to "ice" Wojokowski—create added pressure on him by making him ponder the upcoming kick—the 49ers had already called one time-out. Rules prohibited them calling another. Daniel could feel his tension mounting, as though he were going to kick.

The head referee whistled the ball "in play," and the players got into their stances. Wojokowski, a left-footed sidewinder, crouched slightly off to the right of where the ball would be held for him. The Bears center snapped the ball to the holder, who spotted one end of it onto the turf. Wojokowski sprung forward and met the ball squarely with his left foot, sending it high over the onrushing 49er linemen. It flew end over end toward the distant goal post, traveling with such velocity that the swirling wind had little effect. As the ball went cleanly between the goal post uprights, referees heaved their arms skyward, signaling the kick good. The final gun sounded. The Bears had won 20 to 19.

Almost en masse, the Chicago tour participants surrounded Daniel. They lavished him with warm handshakes, hugs, backslaps, and accolades as if he had just kicked the winning field goal.

⚬◉⚬

On the day following the game, Daniel stood on a bluff above the Pacific Ocean. He couldn't help smiling at the memory of earlier that afternoon when he'd seen off his Chicago tour group at the airport. Again, they'd bestowed congratulatory handshakes, hugs, backslaps, and accolades. All the attention prompted him to remind several of them that he didn't play in the game but had merely organized the tour. He did laughingly promise, though, that if they repeated the trip in the future, he'd get into top shape and *would* kick the winning field goal.

Once the plane departed, he drove to a restaurant near the beach for an early dinner. Afterward, he went for a walk, eventually coming upon the spot where he now stood. Earlier, before twilight had turned into total darkness, he was able to make out a series of fogbanks in the distance, hovering over the endless ocean. Although it was cold, with the wind howling like at the game, he stayed there, virtually mesmerized by the scene. Or was he simply feeling numbed by all the recent developments in his life?

Four days had elapsed since Christina's startling proposal, yet he hadn't come close to integrating it. Sure, he loved her. And he wasn't against marriage. All the more, because it was a major step forward, away from his former life and all his sordid activities. But he knew that his past, and her past, weren't going to just vanish.

His thoughts turned to Alfredo. Specifically to Lawson's suggestion of adoption. Sure, he cared for the boy. Whether it would work was another matter. And was he, Daniel, ready for that type of commitment, together with the obvious responsibility accompanying the imminent birth of his child?

Tara was the next person on his agenda. Although his ex-wife had made it clear that she, Tara, wasn't to be part of his life, Tara seemed to have other ideas. First, college in the San Francisco area, then who knew what? Maybe some type of significant reconciliation? At the very least, it appeared that he'd better not completely exclude her from any plans.

For some reason, Dark Star entered his mind. Not that there was anything to resolve with him. Still, Daniel couldn't avoid the symbolism—Dark Star represented home and family.

Clearly, all the elements for home and family were there. Which led him to some troubling questions. Was he up to it? What made him think he could succeed now when he had failed so miserably in the past? Wouldn't he simply lapse into the same self-destructive behavior he'd fallen into back then, and even fairly recently?

A seagull shrieking overhead interrupted his thoughts. In the dark, the beautiful scene was no longer visible. He knew the ocean was down below only because he could hear the surf pounding toward shore.

He glanced at his watch. Six-thirty. He turned and headed quickly toward his car. He'd have to hurry to get home in time for Christina's seven o'clock call.

·◦✦◦·

"Spoke with the adoption people today," Lawson reported.

"Oh?" Daniel responded.

"They said it would help if you and Christina were married."

"Funny you should bring that up," Daniel chuckled. "I was just about to invite you to the wedding. As my best man."

Lawson looked surprised. The two of them were sitting in a booth, having another dinner together. This one was at a Mexican restaurant, with a couple of mariachis playing in the background. Like at their other dinner, as they ate, Daniel was fascinated by Lawson's ability to wield knife, fork, and spoon with his single hand.

"So, you proposed," Lawson conjectured.

"Not exactly."

"She propose?"

"Not exactly," Daniel laughed at his own redundancy, and at how the topic of marriage had come about with Christina.

"When's the wedding?" Lawson asked the obvious question.

"In about four weeks. Christmas Day."

"Where?"

"In jail."

"In jail!" Lawson guffawed. "How romantic."

Daniel shrugged. He probably would have shown plenty of embarrassment, except the mariachi twosome came over to their table, providing a welcome interruption. Lawson quickly gestured them away.

"You look nervous," Lawson went on.

"What?" Daniel asked, not sure he heard right, above the music.

"You look nervous," Lawson spoke louder.

"I am," Daniel admitted.

"Don't be," Lawson consoled, grinning while reaching out and patting Daniel on the shoulder. "I'll be there."

⚜

"I got some good shit, little lady," whispered the inmate, a large muscular woman, fortyish, dark, and of unclear origin.

Christina turned up the water on the dishes she was washing in the jail kitchen and pretended not to hear her. She knew from experience in prison that one could often ignore something and have it go away. She also knew about this particular prison, having served her prior term here a couple of years earlier. She even knew the inmate from then, since she began a term just before Christina's ended.

That previous time taught her a lot. Always keep a low profile. Make yourself invisible, if possible. Never take a definite position on anything. An attractive young woman, even one more than seven months pregnant, was an inviting target for the advances of other prisoners and guards alike.

Christina could feel the inmate's eyes on her. She began to scrub a pot. The room was very hot and her gray uniform stuck to her skin, so she welcomed a little water spraying off the pot onto her. She certainly didn't like it here, doing kitchen detail, but there were lots of worse assignments. The bathrooms, for instance, where she'd worked during her last term.

"Didn't hear me, little lady?" the inmate persisted.

Christina still pretended not to hear.

"Turn off the fucking water," the inmate ordered loudly.

Christina obeyed. No sense antagonizing her over something as small as water noise. The room became noticeably silent, almost oppressively so. Christina could even hear her breath.

"Now, little lady. Did you hear what I said?"

"About the water?" Christina evaded innocently. "It's off."

"Not about the damn water," the woman whispered harshly while glancing over her shoulder to make sure a guard wasn't around. "About some good shit."

"Oh."

"I got some."

Again, Christina didn't reply. She felt like turning the water back on, even if that made the woman angrier. Anything to create a little noise, since the silence was awful.

"I'll be in the toilet," the inmate hissed. "You sit down beside me."

After drying a dish, the woman left the room. Christina remained behind, thinking. Thinking about how she'd managed to stay off drugs for more than a month. About the wedding only a couple of weeks away. Why take chances now, with everything falling into place? Just yesterday, for example, the prison supervisor had given final approval for the wedding.

A minute or so later, she began walking toward the bathroom. No way could she do anything except join the inmate. Ignoring her would mean standing next to an enraged prisoner in a room full of knives and other dangerous instruments. True, this was a minimum-security jail housing only supposedly harmless prisoners, yet why tempt fate?

Passing a guard in the corridor, she pointed to where she was headed. At least there was a little fresh air along the way, instead of the kitchen's stale heat. Reaching the bathroom, she paused and looked inside. The woman sat in the center of the room, on one of about twenty toilets, all of which were unshielded and in plain view of anyone coming in.

Christina eased down her uniform pants and sat next to the inmate. Neither of them spoke right away. No doubt it would have looked odd, to anyone happening in, to see the two of them side by side when so many other toilets were available. Christina hoped that the inmate wasn't stupid enough to have the drugs on her, because any guard would have been suspicious and probably frisked them on the spot.

"You got money to buy?" the woman asked, muffling her words with a simultaneous toilet flush.

"Short right now," Christina answered softly, almost apologetically.

"Then why the shit did you have me come all the way down here?" the inmate scowled.

She got up, pulled up her pants, and flushed again. Still scowling, she headed off. Christina sat there alone, lingering, allowing the inmate time to cool off. Maybe she should have consented to buy at some future time and place. Placate the woman that way. But even that was risky—sooner or later, she'd have to deal with her.

Not that she wouldn't love to have some decent stuff. As usual, stopping hadn't been easy. Yet, at least she'd been through it before, and this time had the good sense to cut back well before coming here. It very much helped that she now had other things in her life besides cheap hotel rooms and her pipe.

Finally, after flushing the toilet herself, she got up, hiked up her pants, and headed back to the kitchen. On the way, in the corridor, she passed the same guard that she'd gone by earlier. When she reached the kitchen, the inmate didn't say anything, so Christina quietly resumed washing dishes. She didn't so much as glance in the woman's direction, afraid that even that would provoke some type of retaliation.

"Tell me, little lady," the inmate finally broke the silence.

"Yes?"

"You got things to look forward to."

"I do," Christina nodded.

"I dig that," the inmate smiled.

Neither of them spoke again. When the dinner bell rang about twenty minutes later, they left the kitchen separately.

❦

It was ten o'clock at night, and Daniel was tired, but he felt satisfied as he exited the Union Square department store he'd been shopping in. He'd been able to get gifts for everyone on his Christmas list. Several for Christina. A couple for Alfredo. One each for Lawson, Tara, and Stacy, his other daughter. He knew the latter two weren't likely to get past his ex-wife, but he had to try. He even managed to buy something for Dark Star—a canine sweater for cold night walks.

With the number of gifts he was carrying, all in a large plastic bag, he wished that he'd parked closer. That had been impossible, though, because it was the final Saturday before Christmas, and downtown had to endure the double whammy of last-minute shoppers plus the normal restaurant and theater crowds, thus taxing parking lots and street space beyond capacity. He was lucky to have found what he did, almost a mile away.

As he began the long trek to his car, he looked for a cab, but none was in view. At least the evening was pleasant, if somewhat foggy. The sounds and sights of Christmas were everywhere. Carolers and bell jinglers peopled the sidewalks. All the business establishments had their own elaborate decorations. And a live band from nearby was playing Christmas melodies.

As he walked on, the crowds diminished, and the surroundings turned grim. Beer cans littered the ground, and graffiti marred building walls. He started to feel strange. And then he realized why. He'd taken this very same route his first night in San Francisco. And he hadn't been in this type of rundown neighborhood for seven or eight months, not since he and Christina began living together. Why hadn't he recognized where he was when he walked from his car to the department store? Maybe he was just so intent on the shopping he wanted to do that it just didn't enter his mind.

As had happened that first night, he came upon a woman wearing a skin-tight pantsuit at a street corner. He skirted her, without either of them uttering a word. Suddenly he felt cold. As best he could, hindered by the bag of gifts, he pulled his heavy brown coat tight around him, the same one he wore that night. Then he continued.

"It's you," a female voice hissed.

He turned slightly and saw her standing in shadows near a hotel awning. It was the woman in black, who handcuffed him that first night. She had her hands on her hips, and even in the faint streetlight, he could tell she was glaring at him.

"I know you remember me," she boasted. "No one ever forgets."

He didn't reply. A car horn with a wolf whistle blared nearby, but it didn't divert his attention. She had on the same black outfit she'd worn back then—blouse, slacks, spiked heels. Time hadn't diminished her looks in any way. She was right—all the memories did come rushing back. Besides her handcuffing him, of her slapping him, punching him in the stomach, and leaving him helpless all night in that miserable hotel room.

"Congratulations," she persisted. "On surviving."

He stood there, holding the gifts, not moving, not saying anything. Although just minutes before, he'd been cold, he could feel himself beginning to sweat. A couple of young men ran past, almost hitting him, yet still, he didn't budge. Possibly he regarded near-paralysis as his best tactic until he could decide what to do.

"Maybe I was a little harsh that night," she spoke a bit conciliatorily, surprising him. "Prob'ly a bad mood."

He remained silent, recalling those times he'd looked for her. Those Saturday nights. And here she was on another Saturday night, almost close enough for him to reach out and touch.

He could only grimace at how good she looked. The streetlight appeared to radiate off her, giving her a sort of glow. He flashed back to the hotel room that night, to her standing over him, wearing only black panties and brassiere. The familiar wave passed through him. He blinked his eyes and managed to erase the image.

"I feel better tonight," she assured. "Very good news for you. Might even give you a little . . . Christmas bonus."

She snickered with her last words. Still, he didn't speak. She reached into her purse and pulled out a cigarette like she did that other time.

"Got a light?" she asked.

Instinctively Daniel reached into a pocket, as he did then. He felt a matchbook. But then he stopped himself.

"Sorry," he finally uttered his first word.

With a flick of the wrist, she waved off his apology before taking her own lighter from her purse. Another horn honked, this one repeatedly. Again, he paid no attention.

"Got a different room tonight," she enticed. "Much nicer than the other one."

"Sorry," he repeated.

"You don't need to apologize."

"You don't understand," he managed. "I can't go with you."

"Then you *should* feel sorry," she taunted. "For what you're about to miss."

Forcing himself to finally move, he took two or three tentative steps away from her. The image of her in panties and brassiere returned, though, and for a split second, he wanted to stay. But he knew he wanted other things much more. He wanted to move his life forward, away from the past. With Christina. With the baby. With Dark Star. Possibly with Alfredo. And possibly with Tara, too.

Although he realized he'd never be completely cured from his past, he sensed that Christina being firmly in his life was his best safeguard against falling into that former existence.

He began to walk faster toward his car. The image of the woman in panties and brassiere remained, but he knew he wasn't about to give in. Not on a Saturday night or any other night of the week.

"I *should* have kicked you in the nuts too that night," he heard her call angrily after him.

He was practically out of earshot, however. And he was sure he'd never look for her again. Or for any other woman in this neighborhood, for that matter.

Chapter Fourteen

"You look beautiful in your gown," praised one of Christina's bridesmaids.

"Like an angel," her other bridesmaid chimed in.

"Who ever heard of a pregnant angel?" Christina muttered under her breath.

But she too felt happy with the long, flowing, lavender wedding gown Daniel had bought her, which her bridesmaids had just helped her into. More than happy, however, she felt nervous. From where she was now, inside a holding cell designated as her dressing room, she would soon enter the large cafeteria where all the other prisoners waited, and where the ceremony and the jail Christmas dinner would take place.

She also felt cold. Maybe someone forgot to turn on the heat. Or maybe it didn't work in the holding cell. Or, more likely, she simply had a bad case of nerves.

Another negative—she was tired. Dog tired. She'd been up almost all night, making final preparations. Things like choosing the music, picking flower arrangements, and diagramming where everyone was supposed to be.

Fortunately, a few days earlier, the assistant prison supervisor had helped her recruit a wedding party among inmates, so at least she didn't have to worry about that at the last minute. A former justice of the peace would conduct the ceremony. She was well-suited to help people achieve matrimony since her most recent crime was selling counterfeit marriage documents to illegal aliens. Because the ring bearer was often a child, they'd picked an eighteen-year-old who looked fourteen, in on her third prostitution conviction. The bridesmaids were no saints, either. One, a fortyish overweight woman with an unsightly scar below her right eye, was convicted for writing bad checks. The other—much younger, tall, and lanky—bribed a policeman.

"We'll look silly out there in our prison gear," whined the briber.

"I tried to get them to let you wear street clothes," Christina explained. "Wouldn't go for it."

"Figures," grumbled the check writer. "Everything by the book."

Christina considered pointing out that a wedding in prison wasn't exactly by the book, but she refrained. No, she was more intent on her music coming from the cafeteria. When a recording of a song by Scott Joplin began, she realized only three remained until her entrance.

To try to cut her tension, she visualized Daniel in her favorite suit of his, the navy blue one he'd worn the night they went dancing. He'd look handsome in it and take some of the attention off her. Okay, the lavender gown looked lovely, but no way could it restore her lost figure. Why couldn't she have waited for the wedding until after the baby?

Nor was she so sure marriage was such a good idea under any circumstances. With its incredible confinement. Caring for a husband. And then a baby. Out of jail, back to a tiny apartment. Like when she started with that pimp Salvadore, going from one prison straight to another. Mightn't she be tempted right back to the streets, where at least she'd feel free?

"Stop it," she whispered barely aloud while the lanky briber dabbed a little make-up on her face.

"It's only powder," the inmate answered defensively.

"Sorry," Christina grunted. "Must've been talking to myself."

Indeed, she had been talking to herself, attempting to curtail all the negative thoughts. She knew she wasn't about to go back to the streets. She'd already tried that, for almost a decade, and where did she wind up? In a stinking motel room with a shithead with a knife, her butt in the air. It was time to grow up. Daniel was good for her. And he hadn't asked her to give up a thing, except living on the streets.

The recording of her next song began. Consistent with her varied tastes in music, Elton John sang it. She glanced down at her gown for one final inspection. It looked fine, and both bridesmaids nodded approval.

For some reason, though, she didn't feel worthy. Like all these good things shouldn't be happening for her. Once more, she had to tell herself to stop the negative thoughts. Focus, she nearly spoke aloud again. Focus, like she always did whenever she played Scrabble with Daniel.

Speaking of Daniel, another frightening thought came to mind. What if he didn't show up? What if he got cold feet like she'd heard so many prospective grooms did? Who could blame him if he didn't want to marry a pregnant pipe addict who swore all the time?

And if he didn't show up? She'd be standing out there in front of everyone, humiliated. She hoped that someone would at least alert her and save her the embarrassment.

"You sure I look okay?" she asked the bridesmaids.

"Like a pregnant angel," they both answered, almost in unison.

❦

Christina waited breathlessly with the two bridesmaids at the cafeteria door. The last bars of the final song before her entrance, "Higher Ground" by Stevie Wonder, played. Then "Here Comes the Bride" began, and the three of them slowly walked into the cafeteria. To deal with her tension, she tried to focus on the Christmas decorations throughout the spacious room. She feared that all of the two or three hundred people present were watching her, and she attempted to smile but could feel her facial muscles tighten. Then she saw Daniel. He looked wonderful in the navy-blue suit. So distinguished. He smiled at her. She began to relax. She tried to smile again, this time at him, and was surprised when she did succeed.

She heard someone in the room start to cry. Someone else clapped. Another person clapped. Then there were more claps. She also heard a laugh. Soon the entire room was filled with clapping, laughter, and crying.

Helped by the bridesmaids, she continued slowly, carefully, toward Daniel. He stood in the front of the room on a wooden platform surrounded by one of the flower arrangements she'd picked out. She heard her name called out, people urging her on. When she finally got to Daniel, after nearly tripping over a step up to the platform, he reached out and touched her hand. Everyone stood and applauded. Which only confused her because she had no idea she was the least bit popular.

The former justice of the peace—a large woman in her early fifties, also wearing prison gray—stood at the front of the platform and raised her arms to silence everyone and begin the ceremony.

⋅⟨⊙⟩⋅

"I'm your wife," Christina whispered hoarsely into Daniel's ear as they danced as close together as her condition and the wedding gown allowed.

"You are," he whispered back. "And I'm very proud of it."

She felt herself break into a grin. She also felt tears come to her eyes, tears of joy. Not that he'd be able to perceive either response, since she was nuzzled so tightly against his shoulder, in slow-dance position. As another of her musical selections played, "You Light up My Life," she also grinned at several couples of inmates nearby. They, too, all wearing prison grays, were holding each other close while dancing on the cafeteria floor.

"Daniel, could we sit down?" She abruptly pulled him toward some chairs in the corner.

"Sure. Didn't mean to tire you out."

"It's not that," she uttered breathlessly while sinking into a chair. "It's about our daughter not being very lady-like."

"Moving around in there?" he asked, eyeing her stomach as he sat down.

"I'm afraid she's discovered how to kick."

It was true; this was the first time Christina had experienced this type of discomfort. Until then, she'd suffered hardly any pain at all. An inmate had told her that first pregnancies were always the worst, but there'd been no indication of that so far.

"How do you know our daughter's a daughter?" Daniel asked, smiling at her.

"A boy would've been roughhousing in there long before this."

"Oh."

She could tell by his questioning expression that he didn't quite accept her logic. Likely he didn't want to debate right then, though, because Lawson had come over to join them. She smiled a welcome. In her mind, he'd been an excellent choice for best man, especially since he'd helped her during the ceremony by prompting her through a vow.

"'Fraid they gave me the word," he told them, sounding sad. "Time for us to leave."

"So soon?" she protested.

"Said they got to get everyone back to their cells. Then clean up in here. And they still have visitors waiting."

She made a face, one that she was sure she wouldn't have wanted to see. It didn't seem fair that prison life had to resume so quickly. She could tell by Daniel's wistful look and the way he slowly got up from the chair, that he didn't want to leave.

The guards let her go only to the cafeteria exit with him and Lawson, to say good-bye. Lawson shook her hand and gave her a quick peck on the cheek. Daniel's parting kiss was much more passionate. And he started to linger until a guard tapped him on the shoulder.

She heard her music stop. She stood there briefly and watched him head down the corridor with Lawson, toward the prison exit. He still looked wonderful in the navy-blue suit. Once more, she felt tears come to her eyes, this time at the thought of how nice it would've been to spend the rest of their wedding night together.

When she turned around, she saw that her bridesmaids had stayed to help her out of her gown.

Chapter Fifteen

As they drove north on New Year's Eve afternoon, Daniel marveled at the scene before them. To the right of his Buick, verdant hills lofted to varied heights. The blue Pacific spread out grandly below, to the left.

The road meandered inland, away from the coast. Their destination was Mendocino, a seaside resort about two hundred miles north of San Francisco. Two pastured black and white cows stared vacantly at the car as it passed, and Daniel nearly honked a greeting at them. He noticed horses in the distance and pointed them out to Christina.

"Nice," she said.

"Nice," he concurred. "Exactly my sentiment when you told me they were letting you out a few days early."

"They probably needed the space," she replied dryly. "New Year's Eve is always a big night for jails."

"Lucky me."

His last words perfectly described the way he felt. At her insistence, he hadn't seen her at all during the last few days since the wedding. Newlyweds shouldn't be spending time together in jail, she'd asserted. And a honeymoon was to immediately follow a wedding. So, because a honeymoon wasn't possible until now, their only choice was to pretend the days in between didn't exist. He disagreed, but he knew he'd lose any debate.

She reached out and patted Dark Star, lying in the back seat between the two suitcases Daniel had packed before picking her up at the jail. He still couldn't believe that all he had to do for the wedding was show up wearing his navy-blue suit. She had taken care of every other detail.

He couldn't even bring her a gift. Not due to any prison regulation, but because she'd voiced concern that the sight of even a single present might encourage inmates to spend scarce resources on her.

Of course, her concern didn't prevent his buying several items and putting them into the two suitcases. Among them were various new musical tapes, including Bob Marley's very first album. Nor did it keep him from making a reservation at a Mendocino inn for that night and the next three.

Ahead on the road, a sign indicated a rest area in one mile. She pointed to the sign as they went past. So far, the drive had been very slow, taking almost four hours since they'd left San Francisco via the Golden Gate Bridge. Not only had they encountered curvy topography and heavy New Year's Eve traffic, but, at her request, they'd visited nearly every rest stop along the way. He'd grown alarmed, both at the number of stops and the size of her stomach.

"Maybe going this far away isn't such a good idea," he suggested as they pulled into the rest area.

"Disagree. The prison nurse said it would be okay. And there are hospitals everywhere. Anyway, a wedding doesn't become a marriage until the honeymoon."

"Yeah, but you look like you could pop any second."

"A slim figure," she rebutted, "always makes a pregnant woman look more pregnant."

Once more, he didn't exactly see eye to eye with her logic.

❧

"Wow!" Christina extolled once Daniel had shown her around their suite in Mendocino.

He laughed. Her exultation perfectly described their accommodations. Double the size of their apartment; they included a bedroom with a four-poster bed, Jacuzzi, sizable living room, kitchen, and dining area with a table. Although not new, the furniture was tasteful if slightly short of elegant, and even featured a couple of heirlooms. A porch with two lounge chairs overlooked the ocean. Though not visible in the dark, surf pounded relentlessly down below them.

A light rain had accompanied their early evening arrival. There was some confusion at check-in over whether their reservation covered a dog, but the desk clerk rectified things by simply switching them to a different building. Everything turned out fine when their new locale was amid a secluded grove of trees.

"And you didn't want us to come," Christina giggled while easing into a living room chair.

"This place'll still be here after the baby's born," he shrugged defensively. "It won't fall into the ocean."

"Blah, blah, blah," she retorted, sticking out her tongue at him.

Before Daniel could sit down, Dark Star came over to him, panting. Daniel went into the kitchen, found a bowl in a cabinet, and filled it with water. Dark Star slurped the water down quickly, then returned to him.

"I'm sure he's hungry, too," Daniel told Christina. "What about you?"

"Take it or leave it," she said, opening the palms of her hands toward him. "But our daughter's starving."

He laughed, went to the phone in the living room, and began dialing.

⚬◦⟨◉⟩◦⚬

"Bon appétit."

The waiter's parting salutation found Christina sitting in the same living room chair; her mouth open wide in surprise. Just like when the waiter, dressed in a black tuxedo, arrived ten minutes earlier. After covering the table in the dining area with a white satin cloth, he'd placed their dinner on top of it. He handed Daniel a little package and dropped a dog biscuit into Dark Star's bowl before leaving.

"I didn't see a restaurant around here," she said the second the waiter closed the door.

"There isn't one."

"Then where did all this come from?" she asked, pointing to the table on which was spread seafood, pasta, vegetables, salad, and dessert.

"Let's call it . . . magic."

She smiled. He moved to the table and pulled a chair out for her, then motioned her to it. Once she sat down, he went to their suitcases in the bedroom and pulled out a couple of items. Next, he stood behind her and slipped one of them, a lovely turquoise necklace, around her neck. She grinned up at him, again with mouth wide open.

He edged over to a stereo in the living room and removed from his pocket the other item he'd taken from the suitcases. He inserted it into the stereo. Reggae music began. He returned to the table and sat down across from her.

"That's Bob Marley," she beamed.

"His very first album."

"It's wonderful. Just like the necklace."

"More magic," he winked.

Suddenly she grimaced and grabbed her stomach. This time seemed worse to him than the episode after the wedding. Again, he was concerned about their coming this far.

"Maybe you should go lie down," he urged, getting up.

"You're kidding," she said, raising a hand to indicate she was okay. "And miss my first decent meal in almost two months."

He laughed. Not so much at her comment, but at his recalling how she'd rejected his dinner invitation during their early days, claiming a pathetic appetite. After sitting back down, he unwrapped the little package the waiter had handed him. Inside were two greenish-yellow roses. He put them both into a small vase the waiter had left on the table.

"The magic just keeps coming," she grinned.

They began eating. Because they hadn't played Scrabble for so long, he anticipated she'd want to after dinner. Plus, he feared, smoke her pipe. She looked weary from the long trip, though, so he wasn't sure what she'd want to do.

"I know it's New Year's Eve, but do you think I could entice you into going to bed early?" he asked, once more concerned about her condition.

"With all this," she smiled and held out her palms again, "I think you could entice me into anything. But I don't know how much fun I'd be."

"I promise not to try to take advantage," he kidded. "Not with our daughter in the room."

"I brought my pipe," she informed, introducing another of his concerns. "But I don't think I'll smoke it."

"Oh?" He was both relieved and taken aback. "How come?"

"Don't need to. Not with all this magic."

This time it was his mouth that opened wide in surprise. For some reason, the pounding surf outside sounded even louder than earlier.

⁘

"Daniel," Christina rasped, waking him. "I think . . . it's time."

He jumped up out of bed and started dressing. She was less hasty but managed to dress also. The car was right outside the front door, and he guided her to it and inside. The gentle rain they'd encountered upon arrival at the inn had turned into a steady downpour, getting them wet.

"You don know . . . way . . . hospal," she slurred words disjointedly as he began driving.

"Yes, I do," he replied firmly. "Got directions, just in case."

Indeed, he had. They did go to bed early, as he'd suggested. While she was changing into a nightgown, he'd slipped out of the room, over to see the same desk clerk who'd checked them in. On a map, he'd inked in the route for Daniel. They'd been asleep only an hour when she woke him.

"Fas'," she slurred again.

"Don't talk. I'm going as fast as I can."

No doubt about that. While turning the next corner, he skidded, almost losing control of the car. But he straightened it out quickly and accelerated once more. She was slumped over in the seat beside him and began moaning in pain. The rain limited visibility, making driving difficult.

He took a deep breath. He finally let it out when, up ahead, he spotted the neon hospital emergency sign.

⁘

Daniel had been sitting in the maternity unit lobby for nearly five hours. A white-frocked doctor entered the area. Daniel got up from his seat expectantly, anticipating that the doctor would come over to him. The doctor stopped at a small group of people and began talking with them. When he lingered for several moments, Daniel sat back down.

After completing obligatory hospital paperwork, Daniel had done his best to get updates on Christina's condition. Little information was available, other than she'd been taken to maternity. He'd inquired a couple of times at the reception station at maternity but was simply shuffled back to the waiting area. How mother and prospective newborn were doing remained a mystery. As Daniel sat there, he was growing more and more anxious. No news wasn't good news in this case because, he reasoned, each passing minute increased the chance that there'd been complications.

They arrived at the hospital at about midnight. Daniel had carried Christina in the rain into the emergency room. Fortuitously, a hospital attendant saw him and brought over a wheelchair. Daniel tried to go with them to maternity, but the attendant pointed him to the business office.

Another doctor—this one heavy, about fifty, using a cane and wearing blue scrubs—came into the waiting area. Daniel got up again. The doctor came right over. Daniel spotted a speck of blood on his collar.

"Mr. Stanton," the doctor spoke a bit wearily. "It's a girl."

"A girl," Daniel repeated almost mechanically as if receiving old news.

"Probably the long trip wasn't a good idea. Not an easy delivery."

"My wife?" Daniel said, becoming alarmed. "She okay?"

"She's fine. So is your daughter. Six pounds, eight ounces. Not bad for being a little premature."

Daniel nodded slightly and smiled. He was briefly distracted by a blaring hospital intercom summoning a certain doctor to emergency. Nearby, the other doctor and his group broke into laughter.

"Your wife did lose a lot of blood," the doctor told him.

"But she's okay?"

"She's fine."

"When can I see them?"

"Come back in a few hours," the doctor stated, glancing at his watch. "They're both sleeping now. You look like you could use some rest, too."

Daniel shrugged. The doctor tapped his cane once on the floor. He appeared to be about to leave, then seemed to change his mind.

"Oh," he spoke softly, "you might stop by our blood bank tomorrow and make a donation. We get short this time of year, and you'll get credit on your bill."

Daniel nodded again. He would have loved to have seen Christina and the baby right then, to be sure they were okay. If only for his peace of mind before he drove back to the inn.

"Don't worry, Mr. Stanton," the doctor advised, no doubt reading the anxiety in his face. "Your wife and daughter are fine. Now go get some rest."

Daniel nodded one more time. The doctor extended his hand, and Daniel shook it.

⚜

"Our daughter's beautiful," Daniel enthused while sitting down in a chair next to the hospital bed, beside Christina and the baby.

"Babies are never beautiful the day after they're born," Christina differed as she rocked the sleeping infant.

"Ours is. She looks exactly like you."

"You mean haggard and pale?"

He smiled at her. In truth, she did look exhausted and unusually pale. Since his early-morning exchange with the doctor, about nine hours had passed. Most of which, according to a nurse Daniel had talked with before entering the room, Christina and the baby had spent sleeping. He had visited that morning and decided not to wake them. All he'd managed before leaving then was to kiss Christina on her cheek and get a few peeks at the baby.

"I owe you an apology," she said.

"For what?"

"For ruining our honeymoon."

"Sure," he spoke facetiously, yet kindly. "You planned it this way."

She smiled weakly. The same nurse he'd talked with came into the room. Seeing Daniel, she evidently changed her mind about being there because she turned and left. He gazed at the baby, covered with a blanket, and couldn't believe how tiny she was.

"Besides," he continued, "she was born on New Year's. Isn't that what we predicted?"

"Maybe that's a good omen."

"I think a better omen is . . . she has a wonderful mother."

This time, she smiled again a little more energetically, took one hand off the baby, and touched his arm. The baby began to stir, making a brief noise that sounded like a gasp. She made a fist with a tiny hand. Daniel thought she was about to wake up, but she didn't.

"You sure get lots of practice visiting me," Christina spoke more cheerily than at any time during the visit. "In jail. At hospitals."

"Nothing like a little variety."

"And you're getting pretty good at taking me to emergency rooms."

"Practice makes perfect," he winked.

She snickered, then yawned. Maybe he should leave. Except he wanted to stay. Before he could decide, she spoke again.

"Have you thought of a name?"

"No," he admitted, not having given that matter much priority. "Not with everything that's happened. A few possibilities running through my mind. Nothing for sure."

"I have," she sounded definite.

"Oh? What?"

"Rebecca."

"Re . . . bec . . . ca," he slowly enunciated each syllable, nodding at the same time.

"So, you agree?" she said.

"I agree."

"Tell her."

"Okay." He touched the top of the baby's head. "Hi, Rebecca."

"See, Rebecca," Christina said, looking at the baby, who was still asleep. "I told you you have a good father."

He chuckled and kissed Christina briefly on the lips. She closed her eyes. They remained closed several seconds. The baby stirred again and began to fuss quietly. Once more, she didn't wake up. The same nurse entered the room again. This time she checked a chart next to Christina's bed before leaving.

"How's Dark Star?" Christina asked, opening her eyes.

"He misses you."

"And our beautiful suite at the inn?"

"Lonely."

"Do you think the four of us could spend a night there together?" she sounded surprisingly alert. "Before we have to go back."

"Sure," he grinned and glanced at the baby. "Just because this . . . little thing happened, doesn't mean our honeymoon's over."

She closed her eyes once more. He knew he should go. He kissed her forehead this time, and she didn't even stir. He kissed the baby's forehead too. She acknowledged him with a slight gurgle.

"Good-bye, Rebecca." He waved at her while heading for the door.

❦

"Daniel?" Christina said softly.

"Yes?"

"Are you still awake?"

"I guess so. Unless I'm talking in my sleep."

"You're angry," she sighed.

"Shouldn't I be? You asked if the four of us could spend a night together here in our suite. Not in the same bed."

He could feel her smiling in the dark. Rebecca was sleeping quietly between them. Dark Star was snoring loudly near the foot of the bed, most of his body on top of his, Daniel's, legs.

It was late on the second night after Rebecca's birth. Daniel had picked up Christina and her at the hospital earlier in the day. Tending to Rebecca and Scrabble had been the main activities since, until they turned in an hour or so before.

Daniel wasn't furious, he was merely pretending to be. In fact, he couldn't have been more pleased. The four of them together like this. Like a real family.

The way he felt right then, he pretty much didn't care if he didn't fall asleep at all that night.

⋅◈⋅

"She's your spitting image," Daniel remarked to Christina while glancing at Rebecca, asleep in her lap. "Like you were born again."

"What a great idea," Christina replied. "I'd do much better . . . next time around."

"I don't think you're doing so bad . . . this time around."

"I guess I'm sad," she said. "The honeymoon's over."

That was true; it was almost over. They were driving back from Mendocino late the next afternoon and had already sighted San Francisco and the Golden Gate Bridge in the distance. As on the trip north, Dark Star and the two suitcases were in the back seat. Daniel had finally fallen asleep in the crowded bed the previous night. Christina, conversely, hadn't, no doubt, contributing to her mood.

"Something I haven't mentioned that maybe I should have before this," Daniel transitioned to a new topic. "Lawson keeps bringing it up."

"Bringing what up?"

"A possible adoption," he ventured.

"Oh? Whose?"

"I think you can guess."

"Alfredo?"

"Yes," he affirmed.

"Oh."

"How would you feel about it?"

"I don't know," she answered. "It's kind of sudden, with the baby and everything. Can we talk about it after we get back?"

"Sure."

"He is a good kid," she said. "I really appreciated how he saved Dark Star that night before we had dinner with Lawson and him."

"So, you'd consider it?"

"You want another mouth to feed?" she grinned. "Maybe I shouldn't try to stop you."

"Now that we're married, Lawson thinks we'd have a good chance. He wants to look into it."

The sun was dropping on the horizon, and it shined in their eyes. He pulled down both window visors in the front of the car. He couldn't tell whether it helped her because she was gazing vacantly off into space.

"Anyway," she said, sounding wistful, "every little girl should have a big brother. And I think Alfredo might make a good one."

"I'll let you know how things go," he replied. "I'm sure it'll be a while before we have to make a final decision."

She nodded. Neither of them spoke again right away. She continued to look off in the distance. Meanwhile, Dark Star jumped up on one of the suitcases and growled at a car driving next to theirs.

"Something else I was wondering," Daniel initiated another topic.

"What?"

"Well," he said, searching for exactly the right words.

"Sounds important," she replied, seeming only mildly interested.

"Well, why did you . . . want to get married?"

"What a question."

"It's been on my mind."

"I guess it just seemed right. The baby and everything."

"Right?" he queried. "Or normal?"

"Okay, normal." She both sounded and looked impatient. "What difference does it make?"

"Well . . ." He paused to choose his words carefully again. "Weren't you the girl that scolded me once? Said you didn't want to be . . . normal? Sometimes I think you really do want to be . . . normal."

She didn't reply right away. In fact, she didn't reply at all. Instead, she looked back at Dark Star and petted him. They began to cross the Golden Gate Bridge, which appeared more bright orange in the waning sunlight than it usually did. A couple of tugboats were passing beneath the span.

"She's slept all the way," he commented, changing subjects again and glancing at Rebecca while breaking the silence.

"Have you noticed her chin?" Christina veered from his remark.

"No."

"It looks a lot like yours."

"My meager contribution," he smiled.

"Long as we're talking about serious stuff," she sounded ominous. "Do you still wonder about whether she's yours?"

"No," he frowned, reluctant to open a topic which, in his mind, had no satisfactory resolution.

"We can always take a test. To prove it."

He glanced at her. Next, he looked at Rebecca and briefly at Dark Star, who was now panting in the rear seat. Then back to Christina as she began to rock the baby.

"I don't need a test," he spoke decisively. "To prove how lucky I am."

A slight smile curled Christina's lips. She didn't say anything, but he could tell she understood. They came to the bridge toll plaza, and he slowed the car. Surprisingly, the female attendant gestured them through. Then he remembered—three people make a carpool and don't have to pay the toll.

"And now we get a free ride across the bridge," he laughed, speeding up.

"My meager contribution," she spoke dryly while laughing back.

Once they got away from the bridge, a green sign specified that they were entering San Francisco. Daniel kept looking at it as they passed. Then he shook his head.

"Something *is* bothering me, though." His voice was becoming a little hoarse.

"What?"

"That our baby wasn't born here. In San Francisco."

"Why?"

"You and I met here," he said. "Except for the honeymoon, our whole history's here. Ours is a . . . San Francisco story."

"Yes, my sentimental darling, but you're missing the point."

"What?"

"That what we do isn't exactly by the book."

He glanced at her questioningly without speaking.

"You criticized me for wanting to be . . . *normal*." She furrowed her brow at the word.

"I wasn't criticizing you."

"Whatever. Anyway, you just don't get it. There's nothing normal about us or our history. We're more exception than rule."

Of course, he knew she was right. Probably the only rule that applied to them was expect the unexpected. It now seemed appropriate that she began labor on their honeymoon and gave birth in some remote town in Northern California. After all, they met on the streets. He "proposed" at her hearing. And they got married in jail. Plus, while other couples did *normal* things like go out to dinner or movies or plays, the staple of their relationship was playing Scrabble in a hotel room.

A mile or so from the bridge, they motored up a steep hill. Twilight had descended. At the top of the hill, they encountered a thick fog.

Chapter Sixteen

"Looks like we've got a blue-ribbon daughter," Daniel announced proudly as he came into the bedroom at their apartment.

"What makes you say that?" Christina questioned from their bed, where she was sitting and cooing to Rebecca, who was awake.

"See for yourself."

From a package he was holding, he pulled out a plaque. It had a blue ribbon attached. He held it close enough for her to read the inscription, but her attention was diverted briefly by Rebecca beginning to fuss.

"What's it for?" she asked.

"For being the first baby born in Mendocino this year. And looks like there are some prizes in the package."

He pulled out several certificates and started browsing through them. Rebecca made some sort of whistling sound. Or it may have been Christina trying to vary her cooing. At about the third certificate, he broke into laughter.

"What's so funny?" She craned her neck to see him.

"What a coincidence. We're the grand winners of two free nights in a suite at our beautiful inn. And room service dinners from the same place that sent over our magic waiter."

"You're kidding."

"See for yourself." He pointed to the printing on the certificate.

"I guess the honeymoon isn't over, after all," she giggled.

⁘

Daniel was a little weary when he got home from work one evening during the second week after their return from Mendocino. The night before had been especially difficult, with Rebecca waking up twice for "night feedings," and then for some reason, he hadn't been able to fall back to sleep. Christina welcomed him with a kiss, and they sat down at the kitchen table. Dark Star came into the room, laid down under the table, and Daniel began to rub him behind an ear.

"Rebecca asleep?" Daniel asked.

"Since early this afternoon," Christina answered.

"Making up for last night."

"I guess so."

"We got another letter from Mendocino."

"Probably one more hospital bill," he speculated.

"It *is* from the hospital. But I didn't open it. It's addressed to you."

She handed it to him. He heard rain beginning to patter on the roof and reflexively glanced around for the towel they used to dry Dark Star after they walked him in the rain. It was hanging in its usual spot near the door to the backyard. He opened the letter and began to read. Almost immediately, he put it down.

"Anything wrong?" she asked.

He didn't reply right away. Instead, he looked at his hands. They were shaking noticeably.

"The doctor," he began, his voice quivering slightly. "He suggested I donate blood. I did. It was rejected."

"But why?" She looked alarmed.

"Possible . . . HIV."

"Oh, no! There must be some mistake. What are we going to do?"

"We'd better get tested." His voice continued to quiver. "All three of us. You and me and Rebecca."

She put her hands in front of her, on the table. They started to shake, too.

The next few days were awful. Rebecca continued her regular sleep-depriving nocturnal feedings. Anxiety regarding the possibility of HIV contamination was definitely no sleep inducer either for Daniel or Christina. And the blood tests at a medical clinic weren't the least bit pleasant, Rebecca howling her protest. Also, wondering about results only fueled anxiety.

Now, a couple of mornings after taking the tests, the three of them sat in the medical clinic waiting room. Earlier that morning, Daniel had called the clinic for the results but was told that he could not get the verdict by phone, that they would have to come in instead. Which seemed foreboding, because if none of them had the virus, why not just tell him then and save them all the anguish?

While they continued sitting there silently, so many questions ran through his mind. As they had the past few days. If he had the disease, how long did he have to live? If Christina had the disease, how long did she have? Ditto for the baby. What kind of treatments might they need to undergo? Was the disease an absolute death sentence, as he had heard? Would this mean the end of any intimacy for him with Christina? How ironic—to go from all his frenetic activity the past decade to not even being able to have relations with his wife!

"Mr. and Mrs. Stanton," a thin Hispanic man in a gray frock interrupted his thoughts by calling to them from an open door at the front of the waiting room.

Christina got up with Rebecca right away. Daniel, conversely, was slow to move. It was like he was headed for execution. His own, and his family's. Finally, he followed Christina, Rebecca, and the man into a large room, nondescript except for a high ceiling and dull yellow walls. From somewhere nearby, a radio was playing a country-western song.

The man pointed them to a little cubicle enclosed by plexiglass. Christina sat down on a chair on one side of a desk. She continued to look tense. Again, Daniel was slow to join her. The man sat down on the other side of the desk and opened a file.

"The news isn't good," he said flatly, without even introducing himself. "Except for the baby. She tested negative."

⋅⟨◉⟩⋅

"Why must this have to happen now?" Christina asked.

"I guess that's life," Daniel muttered while shrugging.

"We were doing so well. Beginning to get things right."

He shrugged again. They were in their bedroom, Daniel sitting on the La-Z-Boy with Dark Star, and Christina lying back on their bed, nursing Rebecca. It was a cold, late-January night, with the wind howling outside.

"I'm sure you got it from me," Christina declared.

"Just as likely," he countered, "you got it from me."

"I deserve it. All the stupid things I used to do."

"I did my share of stupid things, too," he insisted. "But nobody deserves *this*."

She finished nursing Rebecca and began to rock her. Rebecca burped quietly. An especially strong wind gust rattled the bedroom windows. Almost simultaneously, Rebecca whimpered.

"I still think you got it from me," Christina contended.

"What difference does it make who got it from who?" He felt himself becoming a little impatient. "The simple truth is we've both got it. And thankfully, the baby doesn't."

Rebecca burped again, this one softer than the prior.

⋅⟨◉⟩⋅

It was a Saturday afternoon in mid-February, and Christina sat off by herself in the local Glen Park branch of the public library. She'd left Daniel at home to look after Rebecca and Dark Star. She felt a little guilty, but she needed to get away. So much time in their little apartment, tending to baby and dog, had rendered her claustrophobic.

She had another reason to be in the library. A much more important reason. She had started on a mission. And she wasn't about to let a single day slip by without making at least some progress on it.

She had several medical books in front of her. In the past, her reading material would have varied. But these days, everything was limited to one and only one topic—AIDS, the killer threatening them. Knowledge was the key. If she could somehow devour every particle of information on the subject, maybe they had a chance to survive.

At least there'd been some good news in the last week or so. The specialist that they went to advised them that Rebecca was in little danger from the virus, especially if Christina stopped breast-feeding her. Also, he'd determined that she and Daniel were both in the early stages of the disease. Their ultimate deaths might still be eight or ten years away. In addition, her connections in the old neighborhood would serve them well. Not for street drugs she'd been buying there for years, but for black-market HIV stuff not yet government approved.

She glanced up from her books. A dealer she had used before was standing at the reference desk. She could tell he spotted her. She looked away immediately, back to her books. Too late, he was coming over. The hooded coat he had on covered what she recalled was a bald head, making him look almost like a teenager instead of the thirty-five or forty-year-old she remembered him to be.

"Hi, Christina."

"Yeah," she replied, trying to be as cold as she could.

"Where you been?"

"Around."

"Find someone else?" he whispered.

"I quit."

"Cold turkey?" He looked like he didn't believe her.

"Yeah," she remained cool. "In jail."

"You know where to find me when you start up again."

He walked away, back to the reference desk. She suddenly felt sick to her stomach. Not because she missed drugs in any way. Not so much at him or anything he'd said. No, she felt sick to her stomach at the whole idea of drugs. At how she had allowed them to take over her life. At how they were so much at the root of the plight she and Daniel were now in.

She tried to fight back her nausea by getting back to her books.

·◦·

"Happy anniversary," Christina said while placing on the kitchen table a small chocolate cake with a single candle flickering on top.

"Huh?" Daniel, confused, uttered as he sat down at the table.

"Happy anniversary," she repeated.

"Anniversary for what?" he asked, fully aware of their wedding, a little more than two months earlier. "Today isn't Christmas."

"No, silly," she answered, looking proud of herself. "Today is the day we met. Exactly one year ago."

"The first time you ignored me?" he smiled. "Or the second?"

"I don't count the first time," she smiled back. "I didn't see you."

"You prob'ly wouldn't have seen me the second time either. If I hadn't made such a pest of myself."

This time, as she sat down next to him, she didn't smile. Or show any positive emotion whatsoever. In fact, while beginning to cut the cake with a long knife, she frowned.

"Daniel . . . What if you hadn't made such a pest of yourself?"

"Meaning?"

"What if you'd given up and moved on?"

"What are you getting at?"

"You wouldn't be sick now," she said emphatically, gritting her teeth.

"We've already been through that," he disputed, clenching and unclenching a fist.

She put a slice of cake on each of two plates in front of them. Rebecca, who'd been taking her afternoon nap in her crib in the bedroom, started crying. Neither of them got up right away.

"Still, it must cross your mind," she spoke softly, frowning again.

"What crosses my mind?"

"That you'd be better off if we hadn't met."

"No, it doesn't cross my mind."

"Ever?"

"Never," he said firmly.

To underscore his point, he took a big first bite of cake. She didn't touch hers. The baby was still crying. Which must have disturbed Dark

Star, because he came into the kitchen from the bedroom, where they'd left him sleeping on the La-Z-Boy.

"Do you really think I'd be better off if we hadn't met?" Daniel continued.

"Right." She glanced down at her slice of cake.

"Well, you're wrong," he declared, getting up to go inside to Rebecca.

⚬◦⟨◉⟩◦⚬

"That you'd be better off if we hadn't met."

Although it was nearly midnight, several hours after the anniversary cake, Christina's words still ran through Daniel's mind. He was on the sidewalk in front of their apartment, just finishing a long walk with Dark Star, who was wearing the canine sweater Daniel had bought him for Christmas. Thinking that the cold night air might offer some perspective, Daniel had left Christina and Rebecca asleep about an hour earlier.

He knew odds were very much against his having acquired the virus from Christina. As he'd told her, just as likely she'd gotten it from him. But what if she had given it to him? Would he actually prefer that they'd never met? Would he trade the abbreviated time remaining with her for longer life expectancy elsewhere?

Bending over to pet Dark Star, he tried to imagine life without Christina, without the baby. All he had to do was allow the single candle on the anniversary cake to send him back exactly one year. To soon after his arrival in San Francisco, following the loss of his home and family in L. A. To when he was spending nights in rundown neighborhoods and sordid hotels. With no prospect of change in sight.

His love for Christina had rescued him. The very quirkiness of their relationship had captivated him. Without her, he had no future. He would have simply kept doing what he'd been doing. Maybe at this moment, he was staring at a death sentence. But exactly one year earlier, before Christina, he had no life. He might as well have been dead.

At the front door, he freed Dark Star of his leash, then followed him inside. Aside from the dog's pattering footsteps, the apartment was completely quiet. Daniel made his way into the bedroom. He struggled in the dark to find his pajamas and to get them on. He considered putting on a light, but he decided against it. Carefully, he tiptoed over to the crib to check Rebecca. She whimpered slightly in her sleep but otherwise seemed fine.

He got into bed with Christina. He could tell he didn't wake her because she kept on breathing very deeply. He kissed her cheek and whispered good night. The room was cold, and he was glad that, in the last week, they bought a warm blanket for the bed. Gradually, he eased his arms around her.

"I love you very, very much," he said softly.

She stirred briefly, although he doubted that she heard him.

PART III

Chapter Seventeen

This story could easily end here. In that era of the late 1980s and early 1990s, that's the way it would end for most couples stricken with HIV and AIDS. After expressing their love for each other, they'd simply live out their days together, until the disease finally did them in. For this story, however, that would be leaving out the most important part.

After finishing high school, I would become directly involved. Mother did allow me to go ahead and pick out a college in the San Francisco area. She wouldn't let me live with Dad, though. So instead, he found a female roommate for me with a little cottage not far from his place. When I first told Mother about what Dad had arranged, she wasn't too eager, but I eventually persuaded her to let me try it.

Unfortunately, my high school grades didn't improve enough. None of the major universities in the area accepted me. I'd have to start at San Francisco City, a community college also not far from Dad. Hopefully, I'd be able to transfer later to Stanford, Berkeley, or, more likely, to San Francisco State, which, according to Mother, had a good reputation for liberal arts.

❧

Mother did agree to let Dad meet my flight at the airport and drive me to my new residence. As I walked through the passageway between the plane and the terminal, a couple of carry-ons dangling from my shoulders, the realization suddenly hit me that it had been four whole years since I'd seen him. My heart started its usual thump thump thumping.

What would he look like? Of course, he'd told me of his illness, so naturally, I anticipated the worst. The photos I'd seen of people with AIDS always made them look so pitiful—aging before their time, frightfully skinny, and needing canes just to get around. I pictured Dad with a cane and shrunken to about half his former weight and didn't like it one bit.

I entered the terminal, which was very crowded. My heart was still thumping away. I couldn't escape the idea of four long years with no contact except for phone conversations. I also couldn't escape the image of a shriveled old man.

I looked for him. I didn't see him. Maybe he wasn't there. Maybe he'd gone to the wrong gate, this poor feeble man with a cane.

And then I saw him, coming toward me. I nearly did a double-take, fearful it wasn't him. He looked nothing like I'd pictured. In fact, he looked much better and much happier than the last time I saw him.

"Tara," he greeted, hugging me. "It's been way too long."

"Dad . . ." I broke down crying.

◦◦◦

"I'm a little confused, Dad," I reluctantly brought up a distressing topic because it was the only way I could clear my mind.

"What is it, honey?" He glanced at me while driving.

"Well . . ." I wanted to choose my words carefully. "You don't look . . . at all . . . ill."

"It takes a while for this thing to take hold," he replied.

"Oh."

"A number of years, in fact, according to Christina," he went on. "She's become the family scholar on the subject. I wish I could get her to quit researching so much, but she's so determined."

I nodded, at least relieved that his time evidently wasn't nearly as short as I'd feared. And that there was good reason for why my eyes hadn't deceived me about his appearance. Although I had other questions about his condition, I decided not to ask them right then.

He was driving me to the cottage to meet my new roommate and help me settle in. He'd already shown me the City College campus, and

I'd liked it. We'd also already driven by his place, which, he'd mentioned, was about halfway between mine and the campus. We briefly discussed whether to go inside so I could meet his family, but we both thought it might be better to wait.

"After you told your mother about my illness," he said as we stopped at a red light, "how did you convince her to still let you come?"

"I didn't have to convince her."

"Really."

"I just never told her," I smiled.

He smiled back at me.

⁘

My first year in San Francisco went very well. I liked the cottage Dad had arranged. It backed up against a canyon and offered a wonderful view of woods and greenery down below. I had my own bedroom, and my roommate Susan and I got along nicely. She also was a student at City College, and we even had a couple of the same classes, enabling us to share notes and often study together. Naturally, I spent most of my available time studying, trying to bring up my grades.

Finally, at the beginning of my second year at City, I stayed overnight for the first time at Dad's place. The occasion was that he, Christina, and Rebecca would be away for a week, and he wanted me to housesit, primarily to keep an eye on Alfredo and Dark Star. Despite his insisting that I get Mother's permission, I didn't even try because I was sure she'd turn me down.

Since Christina hadn't traveled much in recent years and Dad wanted her to while they were still healthy enough, they'd gone off to Hawaii. They both felt that Rebecca, now almost four, could benefit from having her world expanded. They'd invited Alfredo and me to go with them but understood that neither of us really could because of school. Alfredo was now in his junior year at a nearby high school and played on sports teams there. In fact, he often practiced baseball with Dad at a field close by.

"Miss Tara," Alfredo said, approaching me as I sat on Dad's living room couch on a Saturday, the second day of my stay.

"Yes?" I replied, looking up from studying.

"I must go out for a dog-walking job."

"Oh? When will you be back?"

"The job is for one hour, Miss Tara. I will be back at three o'clock."

"Better get a jacket on," I said, hearing wind gusts rattling window-panes. "It's cold out there."

He nodded and went off to his room. When he returned, he was wearing a green jacket. It didn't look warm enough to me, but I decided not to object.

"Where is the job?" I inquired instead.

"It is in the neighborhood, Miss Tara."

"I'll be here when you get back."

I watched him head out the front door. Dad had told me he'd grown quite a bit, something even I'd noticed during my time in San Francisco. He was almost six feet tall and well-built if still a little plump.

He had been an official family member for about three years now, since his adoption became final. Around that time, Dad bought this house, a four-bedroom craftsman in the same neighborhood as their former apartment. Christina loved it because it had a large backyard, especially for San Francisco, and she could still walk to the Glen Park village and library.

Once Alfredo left, I settled in to study some more. Dark Star came into the room and jumped up on the couch beside me. I rubbed one of his paws, and he curled up against my leg.

I heard the screech of car brakes outside. At first, I didn't think any-thing of it because the street in front of the house sometimes got busy. Then I thought I heard Alfredo's voice above the wind. I got up, went to the door, and opened it.

I was horrified by what I saw. Alfredo, facing away from me, was crouched in the middle of the street, next to a stationary car. A man, maybe the driver, was huddled over him. It wasn't easy to see because the wind made my eyes teary, but I was sure Alfredo had been hit.

I rushed toward him. In my panic, I must have yelled to him, since he shifted in my direction. I saw alarm in his eyes, validating my emotional state. Then I saw a very small, thin brown dog in his lap. Alfredo said something, but with the wind, I couldn't make out what it was.

"Are you hurt, Alfredo?" I heard myself shout.

"I am okay," he shouted back. "It is the dog, Miss Tara."

"The one you were supposed to walk?" I asked a needless question, confusion my only excuse.

"No, no. This dog, he ran into the street."

"I hit him," the man said, pointing at the car, which was old and gray. "He came out of nowhere."

The guy was Asian, short, thin, and maybe in his early twenties. He was shaking, either from the cold and wind or from the accident. I leaned over for a closer look at the dog. He was nuzzled against Alfredo's chest, and Alfredo rocked him like a baby. The dog's eyes were closed. He was breathing, though in short, quick wheezes. He must have been in pain or shock. I touched him. His short hair felt cold.

"Where is he hurt?" I asked hoarsely.

"The leg," replied Alfredo, clearly much calmer than I was. "I think it is broken."

He nodded toward the left hind, which was splayed out in what seemed an unnatural position. A car came up behind the stationary one and squeezed by it on the other side. I realized we had to do something— about the dog, about all of us being in the middle of the street.

"We must take him to the hospital," Alfredo beat me to any sugges-tion. "I know one that is very close."

"I'll drive you," the Asian guy offered.

꧁꧂

"We'll have to operate," the veterinarian spoke solemnly while glanc-ing up from the small brown dog, who was lying on a large white table. "Or he won't make it."

Alfredo looked at me, and I looked at the vet, a lean slump-shoul-dered man in his forties. We all stood in a small, stark examination room at the animal hospital. The Asian guy, after driving us and waiting a short time, had excused himself to go to work. We thanked him for driving us.

At least the dog, awaiting his fate while lying there, seemed much more alert and comfortable than earlier.

"How much will it cost?" I asked. "He doesn't belong to us."

"Who does he belong to?" the vet frowned.

"We do not know," Alfredo shrugged.

"To answer your question," the vet sounded official, "I'd estimate at least a thousand."

I looked at Alfredo. His expression showed no emotion. I'm sure mine did—concern. I didn't have that kind of money, and I doubted he did either. I was also sure that Dad wouldn't want to advance so much for a dog he didn't own or didn't even know.

I gazed at the dog. His warm brown eyes appeared to be trying to convey something. The room suddenly felt hot, even stifling. It was better than the cold outside, though.

"I will pay," Alfredo declared, raising his eyebrows.

"What do you mean?" I asked, not believing I'd heard him right.

"I will pay," he repeated firmly.

"How?"

"I have money. From my dog-walking jobs."

"You have that much saved?"

"Yes, Miss Tara. I do."

"Are you sure you want to do this?" I still couldn't believe I was hearing correctly.

"I am sure, Miss Tara," he spoke decisively.

"Well," the vet said while seemingly deliberating as he looked at Alfredo. "Since you don't own the dog, maybe I can get the hospital to give a discount. And I could reduce my fee for the surgery."

"That would be nice," Alfredo smiled.

Alfredo and I walked out of the exam room into the hospital lobby and began the paperwork necessary for the operation. He soon left. Although late, he still had his dog-walking job to do.

◦❀◦

The day that Dad, Christina, and Rebecca got back from Hawaii, I told Dad of the accident and Alfredo's generosity in saving the dog. Despite Alfredo's protests, Dad promptly reimbursed him for the cost of the operation. Once the dog was released from the hospital, Alfredo took him to an animal shelter.

Alfredo had become a regular volunteer at that shelter, so he knew of its reputability. He insisted that the dog remain there for at least two weeks, the shelter's requisite "waiting period" for an owner to come forth to claim his or her missing dog. If the owner did not come forth during that time, the dog would become eligible for adoption by a new prospective owner. Alfredo had even gone to the extent of combing the neighborhood around Dad's house to see if anyone knew who the dog belonged to. But no one was able to help him.

The morning after the two weeks was up, Dad, Rebecca, and I headed for the shelter. On the way, Dad mentioned that this shelter was the very first one he and Alfredo visited years earlier, soon after he became Alfredo's "big brother." Because it was his regular day to volunteer there, Alfredo told us to look him up when we arrived.

We found him cleaning out the cage of one of the dogs. He waved to us, put aside a broom he was using, and led us to another cage. There, the little brown dog came to the front of the enclosure. Like at the hospital the afternoon of the accident, his warm brown eyes seemed to be his primary means of communication.

Alfredo opened the cage, attached a leash to the dog's collar, led him out, and motioned us to follow. Dad took Rebecca's hand, and all of us went down a long corridor. Rebecca had on cute little blue jeans and a yellow top, reminding me of outfits I'd seen Christina wear. With her pretty face, brown eyes, and long dark hair, she was unmistakably Christina's daughter.

Several dogs howled or barked at us as we walked, no doubt seeking equal treatment from Alfredo. He signaled to a couple, perhaps conveying they'd get their turn, too. The little dog limped noticeably, but it was clear that his hind leg had healed enough for him to get around.

"I teach him a trick," Alfredo told us as we reached a fenced grassy area near the entrance to the shelter.

He took a rubber ball from a pants pocket and tossed it a short way. The dog, who I recognized as being at least part Jack Russell terrier, darted after it with quick exaggerated movements. I admired his feistiness, first for overcoming his serious injury, and now for disregarding it while chasing the ball and picking it up with his mouth. Using the same exaggerated quick movements, he brought the ball back to Alfredo, dropping it at his feet and eagerly looking up at him for another chance. I glanced at Dad and then at Rebecca, who appeared entranced by the dog.

"What do you think, honey?" he questioned her.

"Can we keep him, Father?"

"I don't . . . knooooow," he drew out the last word.

"Please, Father."

"What would we name him?"

"Let me think." She kept eyeing the dog while cutely pointing her right index finger to her right temple. "What about 'Snappy?' 'Cause he moves so quick."

"That is a good name," Alfredo chimed in, a big smile on his face.

⚜

"I'm pretty sure I know what happens next," Rebecca interrupted the fairy tale I was reading her.

"Really," I answered, having no idea myself.

"Let me think a minute." She displayed that cute habit of pointing an index finger to her temple.

"Okay."

I put down the book. I'd chosen an old Japanese fairy tale called *The Monkey and The Boar*. Dad and Christina had gone to a movie. Alfredo went to a friend's house to study. I'd offered to come over and stay with Rebecca. Once she put on her pajamas and climbed into bed, I'd begun the story.

In the tale, a man was unhappy with his monkey, who was getting too old to do the tricks the man earned his living from. The man contacted the local butcher to do away with the monkey. The monkey, learning of his fate, consulted a boar. The boar devised an intricate plot in which he would kidnap the man's baby, then turn him over to the monkey for safe return to the man, who would therefore be forever grateful to the monkey and consequently spare his life.

To the point where Rebecca interrupted me, everything had gone according to plan. The monkey got the baby from the boar and returned him to the man, who was predictably grateful and promised to spare the monkey. The butcher arrived at the man's home, for instruction.

"Well," I said to Rebecca, who continued to ponder. "What happens next?"

"I think," she replied, "that the boar is in danger."

I smiled at her and went back to reading. As I sat on the bed, next to Rebecca, Snappy came into the room and jumped up into my lap. That surprised me because he rarely left Dark Star. Another surprise, rather than bonding with one or more of the household's human members— Alfredo, his savior, clearly the most deserving—he'd become Dark Star's constant companion. When I reached the final part of the tale, I felt another smile cross my face.

"Bring us some boar meat tonight," the man instructed the butcher in the last line of the story.

Rebecca giggled, sat up in bed, and clapped her hands. Obviously frightened by her reaction, Snappy jumped out of my lap and off the bed, then scurried out of the room. I could only laugh. Not because of the boar's fate or Snappy's response to Rebecca, but since I sensed that this wasn't the first time she had guessed an ending. Yet I couldn't help being a little suspicious.

"You've heard this story before," I slightly accused.

"No," she shook her head, a serious expression replacing the giggles.

"How'd you figure it out, then?"

She shrugged. Her way of shrugging was cute, too. She'd raise her shoulders as high as they'd go, with her arms tight to her sides. And she'd also wiggle her nose innocently.

I'd observed Christina working with her a lot. She'd already started her reading and spelling and even taught her Scrabble. In addition, she read her plenty of stories. Maybe, I concluded, there was a basic format to these fairy tales that would help anticipate endings.

Regardless, I still felt a little silly. I hadn't the slightest clue myself as to how the story would end.

Chapter Eighteen

Christina had been after me for some time to go with her to one of her reincarnation meetings. Finally, one rainy February night when I didn't have classes the next morning, I went. Only about fifteen persons were there, a number no doubt diminished by the weather. She'd warned me that the meetings took place in a dark, drab, and musty community center near Market Street, and her description couldn't have been more accurate.

I found myself yawning a lot through the evening, and almost wishing I hadn't come—until an unusual-looking young man got up to address the circle of people. He had a short, squat frame, suggesting a small square head, yet his head was long and thin, almost pointy, with eyes so close together they practically seemed like one. I was so struck by his odd appearance that I didn't even hear his words at first.

"There was a blinding light," he said, his intensity finally getting my attention. "Then I came upon several wise souls. Master spirits, they called themselves. They were my guides."

"And then what?" asked the balding elderly man that Christina later told me had been the leader for many years.

"And then my soul re-entered my body. I came back to life. I realized I would live some more here on earth."

The guy sat down. I rolled my eyes at Christina, sitting on my left, but she didn't see me. Instead, she got up. I was surprised when she began to speak.

"I have a question."

"Fire away," the leader encouraged.

"Is there any possibility that the soul can leave the body before the body . . . expires?"

"You know from being here," he scolded, "that it happens all the time."

"I mean way before the body expires," she said, hands trembling.

"You mean like years before?"

"Yes. Like years before."

"No, not according to current theory."

"So, a soul can't vacate a diseased body." Her hands were still trembling.

"Right. Not according to current theory."

"Maybe my soul has a mind of its own," she muttered to herself while sitting down.

She looked upset. Almost without my realizing it, the leader got up and headed for the exit. The meeting was over. Christina continued to look dismayed. We sat there a minute, with neither of us saying a word. Then, still silent, she rose from her chair and led me outside.

It was raining steadily. I'd brought an umbrella—she hadn't—and we shared it on our way to Dad's Buick, which she'd driven. As she drove off, we still didn't speak. Finally, while we ascended a steep hill, I broke the silence.

"You raised an important subject."

"It's been on my mind." Her tone was subdued.

"Something's been on *my* mind."

"What?" she asked, turning toward me.

"Rebecca," I said cautiously. "Does she know?"

"About your dad and me?"

"Yes."

"No. Your dad thinks she's too young."

I nodded, although I wasn't sure I agreed. We stopped at a red light. The rain seemed to be coming down harder. I thought I might give her my umbrella when she dropped me off, because I had another at the cottage, and I knew Susan had a couple.

"Anyway," she went on, "she'll probably figure it out."

"Speaking of figuring things out," I changed the subject a bit. "Ever read her the fairy tale *The Monkey and the Boar?*"

"No," she answered as the light became green, and she resumed driving.

"What about in her class? Now that she's started school."

"I doubt it. But maybe."

"She guessed the ending. And I had no clue."

"No surprise," she replied, turning toward me again. "She always beats me to endings too."

"I'll challenge that word, Rebecca," Christina declared, although there was some doubt in her voice.

"Okay, Mother."

Rebecca grinned a little mischievously as if she knew that the word she'd played on the board, "jarl," was good. The "j" was on a triple letter score, so she'd get 27 points, provided of course, that the word stood. If it did, she would take the lead very late in the game.

Christina riffled through a Scrabble dictionary. After reaching the right page, she shook her head. I could tell that it wasn't because the word wasn't good.

"Your turn," she muttered, acknowledging the penalty of loss of her turn for the failed challenge.

"I know, Mother. Don't be a bad sport."

I could only laugh at their interaction, which I'd witnessed many times before. It was often hard to tell which one was the parent and which the child. Regardless, they were together so much that seemingly they could read each other's minds.

"No more letters, Mother," Rebecca reported as she took the last one from the bag.

"How many do you have left?"

"Five. What's the score?"

"362-354." Christina looked miffed once she'd tallied on the score-pad in front of her.

"Who's ahead?" Rebecca spoke like she knew.

"You are."

The three of us were sitting at the kitchen table, Christina and Rebecca across from each other, with me in between. I'd joined them midway through the game. It was Thanksgiving morning, and Christina had gone to the stove a couple of times to check on the turkey she was roasting.

Dad entered the room, followed by Dark Star and Snappy. It was clear that his disease was beginning to show. The same could be said for Christina.

At this point, I need to say that my narrative will not be describing their symptoms in any significant detail. I loved them both too much to do that and want always to remember them in their healthier states. Besides, this story isn't about AIDS symptoms, and anyone interested can look them up in any medical encyclopedia.

"Happy Thanksgiving, everyone," Dad said cheerfully.

"Happy Thanksgiving," I replied.

"Smells good in here." He sniffed at the stove. "When do we eat?"

"Just like a man, Father," Rebecca groaned mockingly. "When do we eat? I suppose you'll want one of Mother's wonderful spaghetti dinners after the turkey."

"Not a bad idea," he commented.

"Your turn," Christina addressed Rebecca sourly.

"Sounds like someone's unhappy because they're losing to a six-year-old." He glanced over Christina's shoulder at the score-pad.

"I'm almost seven, Father," Rebecca bossily corrected.

"Are you going to play, young lady?" Christina asked, pretending to be angry at Rebecca. "Or are you going to chatter all morning?"

I'd become used to this sort of family repartee. That was because I'd become an official family member about two-and-a-half years earlier when Mother finally relented and allowed me to move into the house. Susan had transferred to UCLA in Los Angeles, and I was without a roommate. But my grades, almost straight A's my second year of community college, had been my most compelling argument. I also think she'd softened toward Dad, realizing, from my reports, that he had been a positive influence on me and had turned his life around. Naturally, I didn't dare tell her of his illness, fearing that would cause her to change her mind.

I'd transferred to San Francisco State, a lovely campus near the southwest edge of the city. I'd done well there and, in fact, recently started grad school, studying English. I could have applied to Berkeley, but that would have meant a long commute unless I lived on or near campus. I was happy in the house, for years had wanted to live close to or with Dad, and I wasn't about to give that up.

Rebecca attached "curv" to an "e" on the board to make "curve." Since sitting down with Christina and Rebecca, I'd marveled at Rebecca's Scrabble performance. Despite my not being sure of its definition, the word "savant" kept coming to mind—not as a potential Scrabble play, of course, but as an explanation for her talent.

"Double word score," she announced. "Twenty points. What's the score now, Mother?"

"382-354," Christina grumbled.

Alfredo came into the kitchen. He patted both dogs. As usual, Snappy promptly shuffled away from him. He'd never warmed up to Alfredo. The only reason I could give was that despite his leg having completely healed, he still associated the car accident and resulting injury with Alfredo. Or it could have been the subsequent operation, or the animal hospital, or the dog shelter afterward. Alfredo didn't seem to mind, though, as if he understood.

Alfredo had followed in my footsteps by going to City College and then transferring to San Francisco State. He took as many pre-med classes as he could, his eventual goal to become a veterinarian. At both places, he played on the baseball team. Dad continued to practice with him whenever his health permitted, and Dad rarely missed a game.

Christina used six of her seven letters to make "candid" by attaching the second "d" to the "e" on "sire," already on the board. She got eighteen points, reducing Rebecca's lead to ten. I wondered whether Rebecca had ever beaten her but hesitated to ask because they were both concentrating so hard.

"C'mon, Alfredo," Dad said. "Let's go inside and watch some football. Doesn't look like us *men* are much wanted in here."

Alfredo nodded. The two of them left the room. Surprisingly, with the aroma of food so strong in the kitchen, Dark Star went too, naturally followed by Snappy. I chuckled inwardly at the thought that Dad's comment about men had influenced them also. Regardless, I soon heard an announcer from the living room TV talking about football.

Rebecca fidgeted with her one remaining letter. All she had to do to win was play it. She scanned the board carefully. A look of frustration crossed her face.

"Pass," she said.

"Got a 'v' left, huh Rebecca?" Christina needled her a little.

"I'm not telling, Mother."

For a second, Rebecca looked like she might stick out her tongue at Christina. I peeked over and could see that Christina was right—Rebecca did have only a "v" left. I knew enough Scrabble to know that it was a difficult letter to play, especially by itself, at the end of a game. If she got stuck with it, Christina would get eight points for double its value, four. Christina, herself, also had only one letter left. If she could play it and get at least three points, she would win.

I wondered if she might consider letting Rebecca win. I watched her closely for any indication as she studied the board. I could almost see the wheels turning in her mind. My curiosity mounted, along with the suspense.

"Ever beaten her?" I couldn't keep from finally asking Rebecca.

"Never." She scrunched up her face while squirming in her chair.

"And she's not going to beat me now," Christina spoke with determination.

She put her last letter on the board, an "n," next to an "i," to make "in" for two points. The game was over. Christina tallied the final score.

"382-382." She looked directly at Rebecca. "You didn't beat me."

"No, Mother," Rebecca answered, looking back at her. "But you didn't beat me either."

This time Rebecca did stick out her tongue at her.

⁘⧉⁘

I heard barking. From the nervous high pitch, I knew it wasn't Dark Star. Nor could it have been Snappy, because he never barked. Alfredo must have brought home a new dog from the shelter to play with our two.

The barking continued, and I became a little concerned because Dad and Christina had gone out to visit a sick friend that evening and left me in charge of Rebecca. I got up from my bedroom desk, where I'd been studying. The barking grew louder and more insistent, even frantic.

"Miss Tara, Miss Tara, come quick, come quick." Alfredo's voice registered urgency above the noise.

"What is it?" I shouted back.

"It is Miss Rebecca." He practically ran into me at my bedroom doorway.

I saw fright on his face, which greatly alarmed me. He went rapidly down the hall, and I hurried after him. The barking grew even louder and more frantic.

When we entered Rebecca's room, I immediately panicked. Clad in green pajamas, Rebecca was rolling around on the floor, in obvious distress, coughing uncontrollably and choking. Snappy was feverishly circling her. He had been the barker.

I rushed to kneel beside her. I pulled her close. She continued coughing and began wheezing heavily.

"Please, Miss Tara, let me try." Alfredo's expression still showed fright, yet I knew he was much calmer than I was.

I let go of Rebecca and moved aside. Alfredo kneeled above and behind her. He put his hands and arms around her throat and upper chest. I could see him start to apply pressure.

Snappy still circled and barked. Rebecca still coughed and wheezed. I could feel my breath come in short, tense bursts.

Alfredo kept maneuvering. Eventually, something came out of Rebecca's mouth and landed on the floor. I could see it was a chicken bone, which had apparently lodged in her throat.

With his open hand, Alfredo struck Rebecca twice on her back. She began to breathe much easier.

⋅◦⟨◎⟩◦⋅

"We waited up for you," I told Dad and Christina the instant they came in the front door. Alfredo was standing beside me.

"Anything wrong?" Dad asked, obviously sensing our concern.

"Rebecca," I said. "She almost swallowed a chicken bone."

"Oh no!" Christina registered her own alarm and quickly started for Rebecca's bedroom. "She okay? Where is she?"

"She's okay." I tried to act calm. "She's sleeping. We keep checking on her."

"You call a doctor?" Christina paused on her way inside.

"Alfredo was the doctor," I explained. "He saved her."

"I only do what I learn at the shelter," Alfredo spoke almost apologetically. "To help dogs if they swallow something bad. Snappy, he is the one who save her. He find her. He never bark before. I come when I hear him."

"She must have gotten into that leftover chicken in the fridge." Christina seemed a bit relieved. "I'd like to see her."

She started again toward Rebecca's room. The rest of us followed. She went directly to Rebecca's bed and, finding her still asleep, gently woke her.

"You okay, honey?"

Rebecca sat right up in bed. With only dim light coming into the room from inside, Christina turned on a lamp next to the bed. I could see by Rebecca's grim expression that she was upset.

"Why did you let them take me away?" she asked raspily.

"Who, honey?" Dad spoke soothingly.

"I don't know."

"No one took you away," Christina told her.

"You had a little accident, sweetie," Dad continued in his soothing tone. "Nothing to worry about."

"Don't let them take me away again," Rebecca sounded angry.

"Don't worry, honey," Dad consoled.

"And I don't want any of you to go away either."

I watched Dad and Christina glance at each other. They both looked uncomfortable. I hoped that they'd told Rebecca of their conditions by now, but evidently, they hadn't.

"Promise me." She gazed at them sternly.

"Yes, honey?" Dad replied softly.

"That you won't go away."

"We're staying right here with you," Christina said, her tone both vague and sad.

Rebecca looked at her briefly, then away. She laid back down on her pillow.

❦

What happened during the next few weeks was startling. Christina's symptoms—which, as I stated, I won't detail—worsened. Strangely, Rebecca developed identical symptoms, which also seemed to worsen. Dad and Christina, naturally very concerned, took her to the same doctor they'd been seeing. Because it was Easter break and I had no classes at the time, I went too.

"I've seen this before," the doctor said after briefly examining Rebecca. "Nothing to worry about."

"What do you mean?" Christina asked, her anxious expression contradicting the doctor's statement.

"Very simple. It's her way of dealing with things."

"What do you mean?" she repeated, looking no less anxious.

"You know that old phrase. If you can't beat 'em, join 'em."

"I still don't understand."

"Wherever you're going," the doctor declared, "she wants to go with you."

Dad, Christina, and I looked at each other, then at him. He was tall, in his forties, and had quite long hair. He'd spoken in very low tones throughout the conversation, barely above a whisper, so that Rebecca couldn't hear him. She was sitting in a far corner of the examination room, trying to solve a puzzle the doctor's nurse had given her.

"You sure that's all it is?" Christina asked, still looking anxious.

"I'm sure," the doctor answered. "Of course, I can test her if you want. To make certain she hasn't somehow contracted . . ."

"No, that's okay," Dad interrupted. "She's been tested too many times already."

"I assume you've told her about . . ." the doctor spoke in even lower tones.

"No, we haven't," Dad interrupted again, whispering and shrugging.

"I guess you don't need to," the doctor said. "Looks like she's got it pretty well figured out."

Rebecca started walking toward us. She'd finished her puzzle.

Chapter Nineteen

"Wanted to talk with you," Dad spoke as if he had something serious to say.

"Sure," I replied.

"It's about . . . for after."

I could feel myself grow tense. A moment earlier, he'd knocked lightly at my bedroom door. I was at my desk, writing Mother a letter. I thought he'd sit down in a nearby chair, but he didn't, instead preferring to remain standing.

"Lawson's agreed to handle finances," he said.

"Good," I replied vaguely, having no real opinion.

"When it happens," he said, dropping his shoulders a little, "Christina and I have a request of you."

"Yes?"

"Rebecca. We'd like you to be her legal guardian."

Of course, I realized that sooner or later, they'd have to make plans. And I was aware that I might be the logical choice. But I suppose I wasn't quite ready to face this inevitable. I shifted uncomfortably in my chair.

"What about Alfredo?" I asked.

"As Rebecca's legal guardian?" he frowned.

"No, no. I mean, what are your plans for him?"

"Well, we've made financial arrangements. He'll be twenty-one in less than a year. So, a guardian shouldn't be an issue. Otherwise, Lawson."

Dark Star came into the room. As usual, he was tracked by Snappy. They both went right to Dad. He petted each of them, giving me time to think.

No question, I loved Rebecca. Besides her remarkable intelligence, she was a great kid—perky, fun, yet focused. Any prospective parent would adore having her as their child.

But was I ready? I had college to finish and, hopefully, a career to develop. And maybe my own family to start. I had a life of my own.

"I can understand your not wanting to," he pretty much summarized my doubts.

I looked at him. His symptoms were advancing. And Christina was in no better shape. I wondered how much time they had left.

His anguished look expressed how badly he wanted me to accept his request. I thought back to why I'd come to San Francisco in the first place. I'd come to be near him. I'd come to help him if I could. Clearly, he was seeking my help right now in a way that really mattered.

"I'd be honored to be Rebecca's legal guardian," I said. I was surprised by my resolve.

⚬

One evening a couple of weeks later, Dad, Christina, and Alfredo were all away from the house. I took the opportunity to knock at Rebecca's bedroom door, which was slightly ajar. I heard her shuffling around in the room. Then she came to the door and opened it wide.

"Hi, Tara."

"Wondering if we could talk?"

"Okay."

I followed her into the room. I'd seen it many times before; however it was always a fresh sight to me because it was far from an ordinary seven-year-old's room. Oh, it was messy, like one would expect of a seven-year-old, with papers and pictures scattered all over the place. But dozens of books were there too, and I knew from experience that many of them were well beyond children's fare.

"Reading?" I asked, spotting an open book on the bed.

"Yes."

"May I ask what?"

"I suppose so," she shrugged. "One of Mother's books."

"Can I see?"

"I suppose so," she sounded even less eager.

I motioned her over to the bed, and we both sat down. I picked up the book and turned it over, careful not to lose her place. The title leaped out at me—*AIDS, An Epidemic.*

"Your mother give this to you?" I frowned.

"Not exactly," she admitted.

"How'd you get it?"

"Found it in her room."

"She know you're reading it?"

"Maybe."

"Maybe?"

"She's seen me looking at some of her books before." She fidgeted next to me on the bed.

"On this subject?"

"Well, not exactly. On Scrabble. On music."

"This isn't exactly Scrabble or music," I heard myself speak in a lecturing tone.

"You won't tell her, will you?" She raised her eyebrows.

"No, I won't tell."

"Promise?"

"I promise.

"Anyway," she said. "It looks like she's getting tired of reading about this stuff."

"How can you tell?"

"Because every time I pick up this book from her room, her bookmark is in the same place. And lately, I haven't found any other books on this subject in her room."

"Oh," I replied, once more admiring her deductive ability, "I see."

"And you know something else?"

"What?"

"If she's getting tired of this subject, I'll be happy to take over for her."

"Oh," was all I could manage in response.

"Anyway," she continued her clairvoyance, "I don't think this is what you wanted to talk with me about."

"You're right. I do have something else to discuss. Something very serious."

"You're not going to tell me about Mother and Father, are you?"

"What about them?" I probed, although I had more than that in mind.

"You know. How sick they are."

"Did they tell you?" I asked, hopefully.

"No, they didn't tell me."

"Did you figure it out when we went to the doctor?"

"I figured it out way before we went to the doctor."

"Oh."

"What did you want to talk with me about?" she became the prober.

"Well," I began tentatively. "Your mother and father. They want me to be your guardian. For after."

"I was pretty sure that's what they'd do."

"I just want to be sure it's okay with you."

"It's okay with me," she said, crinkling her nose. "On one condition."

"What's the condition?" I chuckled slightly because I'd been around Christina enough to know that Rebecca had just duplicated Christina's standard way of giving in.

"That you'll let me read any book I want."

"We'll make that our little secret," I winked at her.

"Promise?"

"I promise," I said, then gave her a brief hug.

⦁⦿⦁

"Her teacher say anything?" Christina asked, motioning me into the kitchen after I'd walked Rebecca home from school one Indian-summery October afternoon.

"Same as always," I replied. "She's amazing."

Christina nodded. I sat down with her at the kitchen table. She looked especially wan. Although it could've been the heat, I had my doubts. She seemed to be growing frailer. In my new role as a future guardian, I'd taken it upon myself whenever I could to pick up Rebecca from her class, now third grade, and occasionally check her progress.

"Amazing," Christina muttered sadly. "That's what my teachers used to say about me. And look what's become of me."

"Don't be so hard on yourself."

"I don't have much to look back on."

"You do have one thing that's especially special," I said, trying to cheer her up.

"What?" she asked glumly.

"Not *what*. Who."

"Miss Amazing?"

"Miss Amazing," I confirmed.

The sounds of Rebecca playing some music on her tape player came from her room. Christina took a sip of tea from a cup in front of her. I glanced at my watch. I needed to be aware of the time because later that afternoon, I had to attend a writers' workshop, a recommended part of the Ph.D. program in English at San Francisco State that I recently began.

"Speaking of Miss Amazing," Christina said. "She's been reading my books. I've discovered several missing."

"Really," I feigned innocence. "Your books on Scrabble and music?"

"Lately, my books on AIDS."

"Oh," I gulped a little too dramatically.

"You know, for years--ever since your dad and I tested positive--I've been studying AIDS. Keeping tabs on research. Experimental drugs. Possible cures. Every little thing that happens."

"I'm aware of that. I've seen you. And Dad told me when I first came to San Francisco."

"But I'm getting tired of it," she admitted, no question looking the part. "She wants to take over for me, I'll gladly step aside."

"Maybe that's what she has in mind," I acknowledged. "Even though she's only eight."

"Being eight has nothing to do with it," she debated, sounding a bit facetious. "Because as we're saying, she's Miss Amazing."

"Has she shown interest in reincarnation, too?" I changed the subject a little.

"Yes."

"Speaking of which, you remember that meeting we went to? When that guy spoke about coming back to life? And all that stuff about blinding light? Wise souls? Master spirits?"

"Yeah?"

"Well," I said, "it bothered me. All that stuff seemed phony. Made up for effect. Making his whole story seem farfetched to me."

"I understand."

Her focus, however, appeared to shift elsewhere. Specifically, to Rebecca's room, from which reggae music emanated. She cocked her head, no doubt to listen closely.

"That tape," she sounded wistful. "I used to play it for your dad. Not long after we met."

"Oh?"

"Yes. On an old tape player I would bring with me."

"I do want to thank you," I said, again changing the subject a little.

"For what?"

"For all you've done for Dad. For helping him straighten out his life."

"He's done the same for me," she sighed. "I only wish we had more time."

"Me too," I also sighed. "And yet, he does seem content. Even with . . ."

"I think he *is* content," she affirmed. "He's gotten what he wanted. A family."

"And you?"

"I'm not as content. Something's missing."

"What's missing?" I asked straightforwardly.

"What reincarnation offers," she answered directly. "The chance to get things right. Even if some of the stuff *is* phony."

"I understand."

"Anyway, maybe Miss Amazing can get things right for me. I won't have to come back."

"Back where?" I asked.

"Back to life."

I nodded. I glanced at my watch again. It was time for me to get ready to go to the writers' workshop.

Chapter Twenty

As I walked with Mother up a grassy hill that overlooked the cemetery's main part, I could feel my tears well up again. In recent months, they'd been my constant companion. It was a cold, windy mid-December morning about two weeks before Rebecca's tenth birthday, and Mother had on a heavy black woolen coat that I'd never seen her wear before. Although there were no distinct signs visible, the aura of Christmas was definitely in the air.

I had just attended my third funeral in less than a year. First, there was Dark Star, who we buried in our backyard. Then came Christina, laid to rest in this same cemetery. And now, minutes earlier, Dad, in a grave beside Christina.

"Mother, thanks for coming," I told her for about the dozenth time, my voice quivering.

"I'm glad I did," she replied.

"Could I ask you something?"

"Sure."

"Do you think . . . ?" I paused for the right words. "Do you think you could find it in your heart to forgive him?"

"I think," she answered, then paused also, apparently searching for the right words herself. "I think I already have."

"Thank you."

"Seeing you now," she went on, her eyes blinking from the cold and wind. "Seeing Rebecca. And even Alfredo. No question what an influence he had on all of you."

I couldn't keep from crying. We reached the top of the hill. Through my tears, I could barely spot Rebecca down below, wearing a black bonnet and warm yellow coat, standing with Alfredo and Robert Lawson. She left them and began to climb the hill toward us.

I glanced at Mother, who I could tell was watching Rebecca too. In the seven years or so since I'd left L.A., she had aged quite a bit. Her hair had thinned and turned gray. But I still considered her a fine-looking woman and anticipated that someday she'd remarry. Based on her letters, our phone conversations, and the few times I'd visited her, though, she didn't appear the least bit interested.

Rebecca waved to us as she approached. A couple of times during the ceremony, I'd seen her crying also. She got to where we stood at the top of the hill. Mother immediately put an arm around her. Right before the ceremony, I'd briefly introduced Mother to her as her stepmother—a term which no doubt wasn't accurate. Then and now, I could feel an instant kinship between them.

"You don't look *wicked*," Rebecca grinned up at her, of course referring to fairy tale lore and, in particular, to the story of Cinderella.

"You don't know me very well," Mother said with a glint in her eye.

"I hope I get to know you . . . *very well*." Rebecca curtsied slightly.

Even in my sadness, I let out a muffled laugh. Rebecca was already working her magic, and I was sure Mother would revisit us. Or maybe invite us to L.A.

Mother took Rebecca's hand, and the three of us started to descend the hill. I tried hard, but I couldn't avoid another round of tears.

꧁❀꧂

"It feels eerie," Rebecca told Mother and me.

She shook her head as if to rid herself of whatever impulses she was experiencing. It was the final afternoon of a giant weekend science fair at the convention center in downtown L.A., and the three of us were sitting near a refreshment stand in the back of a huge auditorium, snacking on cookies and orange juice. Having turned thirteen less than a month before, Rebecca had started dressing like the teenager she'd become. She had on one of Christina's favorite and most youthful outfits—jeans and a blue pullover top.

"What feels eerie, honey?" Mother asked her.

"Like I've been here before."

"To this expo?"

"Well," Rebecca answered thoughtfully, "sort of."

"But you said this is your first visit to L.A."

"I know," Rebecca agreed, yet her expression conveyed doubt.

"Maybe you're confusing this with some other science fair you've been to," Mother suggested.

"Maybe," Rebecca acknowledged, not very convincingly.

As I'd hoped at Dad's funeral, Mother did invite us several times to visit her in L.A. But, because of both our separate school commitments, we hadn't been able to arrange a mutually acceptable time until now. With the science fair in town, this was an especially appropriate time since Rebecca would soon start high school, where she planned to take as many science classes as possible.

Throughout the weekend, I'd been fascinated by Rebecca's intense interest in everything at the expo. She refused to pass up a single exhibit or demonstration, and she visited many more than once. I had to admit that Mother and I often tired of following her around.

"You know," Rebecca sounded a little disappointed while taking a bite of cookie, "I was hoping there'd be some medical stuff here."

"Medical stuff?" I asked though I had a pretty strong suspicion.

"New ideas," she clarified.

"New ideas?"

"You know," she said, seeming hesitant, "on diseases, things like that."

"You mean like," I asserted, my tone less than kind, "possible cures for certain diseases?"

She didn't answer. She didn't need to. All three of us knew that I'd made my point. And that I'd been a bit harsh in the process.

"I hope you have other interests besides science, honey," Mother followed up on my point in a much gentler manner. "It's important to be well-rounded."

"I know," Rebecca replied a bit guardedly. "I like Scrabble, music . . . And . . . reincarnation."

"Reincarnation," Mother sounded surprised.

"Yeah," I couldn't help being sarcastic. "She goes back and forth between reading . . . science and reading about reincarnation. Real kids' stuff."

"Tara, you're always saying that," Rebecca accused.

"Well, you could lighten up a little."

"My big sister," she said, looking miffed, "sometimes forgets her promises."

"What am I forgetting this time?"

"To let me read whatever I want," she stated, raising a finger toward me.

I shrugged. She took another bite of cookie. A small gathering nearby applauded a demonstration we'd already seen twice. Rebecca gazed around the huge auditorium.

"It still feels eerie here," she said.

⌖

Whenever given a choice between Rebecca studying AIDS or her studying reincarnation, I unfailingly took reincarnation. Consequently, when I observed her reading quite often from a book called *Journey of Souls* during her second year of high school, I kept my promise and didn't object. And when she occasionally requested that we go to the reincarnation meetings at the community center near Market Street, I gladly drove us (we still had Dad's old Buick).

One balmy early-April evening, when we both had spring break and no classes all week, we decided to go. No doubt buoyed by the weather, the crowd was larger than usual—perhaps over thirty. Entering the meeting hall, I noticed that a pervasive paint smell had replaced the regular musty odor. Evidently, a badly-needed fresh coat had been applied recently.

Once we sat down, and the first speaker began, I frequently glanced at Rebecca, next to me. She looked tense, very different from her usual calm demeanor. During the five-plus years since I officially became her legal guardian, I was constantly amazed at her. Not so much at her intelligence, which I'd grown accustomed to, but because she was incredibly self-sufficient. Even well before Dad and Christina died, she took care of herself, seemingly more as a preference than any necessity demanded by their illness.

The first speaker finished and sat down. I was surprised when Rebecca got up. She'd never addressed the group before. I assumed that was the source of her tenseness.

"I'm starting to . . . wonder about something," she began tentatively.

"Yes?" probed the aging leader, the same one who'd been there for years.

"Whether my deceased mother's soul," she sounded a little less unsure of herself, "lives inside me."

"Soul or spirit?"

"Maybe both." She appeared to be gaining confidence. "No question about her spirit. But it feels like there's much more of her than that inside me. Maybe her whole being."

"Say more."

"Well, she didn't have enough time left to finish what she set out to do."

"Elaborate," he pressed on.

"During her last ten years or so--until she got too sick--she faithfully studied the disease that eventually did her in. She was obsessed with finding a cure Or at least finding some kind of remedy."

"That's not unusual for someone who's about to . . . pass on," the leader said after clearing his throat.

"I understand." She briefly looked down at the floor. "And I realize it's not unusual for a child to follow in a parent's footsteps. But I feel *driven* to do what she was doing. Like she's directing me. Like I have no choice. Almost like . . . I've become her."

I was getting upset. Because her hands were trembling, I could tell she was getting upset, too. I was sure she wanted to sit down; however the leader made no move to dismiss her. Instead, he merely paused, probably to reflect.

This gave me a moment to reflect also. Certainly, I was aware of the enormous affinity between Christina and Rebecca. But was Rebecca saying that Christina was living inside her? Or was she saying that Christina was only living through her?

Too bad, I didn't have enough knowledge or understanding of the concepts of reincarnation to evaluate properly. Furthermore, I wasn't even sure I believed in reincarnation at all. Yet I had to admit that what little I did know about it—and what I'd witnessed of the relationship between Christina and Rebecca—made Rebecca's theories seem possible.

"I'd like to hear more," the leader finally spoke.

"Please," Rebecca stammered, obviously still upset. "Not now."

Then she did sit down. Seconds later, she got up again and, nearly stumbling over me, made her way toward the exit. I quickly followed. Once we got outside, I caught up to her.

"You okay?" I asked.

"I think so," she whispered hoarsely.

I put an arm around her. I could feel her still trembling. We walked toward the car, which wasn't too far away. The night air was still balmy, and I hoped it would calm her.

"Want to talk about it?" I encouraged.

"No, Tara." Her voice shook a little.

"When we get home?"

"No, Tara. Not when we get home. I don't think I want to talk about it . . . ever again."

We walked the rest of the way to the car silently. I sensed that not only wouldn't we talk about what happened, but very likely, Rebecca had attended her last reincarnation meeting.

For the first time in many years—probably since one of Christina's renowned spaghetti feasts—Rebecca, Alfredo, Lawson, and I all had dinner together. The restaurant we picked, if old, was elegant, with lustrous dark-wood paneling adorning the walls. Horses were a primary motif; there being numerous photographs, paintings, and bronze statues of them placed strategically throughout. The reason we'd selected this restaurant was that it was the only one near the house we could find open on New Year's Day, Rebecca's seventeenth birthday.

Besides Rebecca's birthday, the occasion for the dinner was that we all had something to celebrate. A city commission had recently honored Lawson for his lengthy coaching career and his ongoing outstanding service to San Francisco youth. Alfredo had started his first full-time position as a veterinarian at the same animal hospital where we took Snappy after his accident.

Meanwhile, I had accepted a position as an assistant professor of English at San Francisco State. What proved instrumental in my being hired was publishing the novel I had started in the writers' workshop there. What began there, eventually became the entire book you are reading.

It wouldn't be fair for me not to acknowledge all the help I received from workshop members, as I wrote. Although they wanted no credit for their efforts, they were incredibly valuable in the process. Since Dad's actions and point of view were integral to the novel, their helping me adopt a less feminine tone and emphasis throughout was beyond significant. And luckily, several workshop participants were sports enthusiasts who assisted with appropriate jargon and description for the sports scenes.

I would never have started the novel without Dad's encouragement. At the project's embryonic stage, he pledged his support. He trusted me enough to write this novel properly and respectfully—albeit realistic—that he willingly provided a wealth of information about Christina and him. He constantly urged and reminded me to use my imagination to fill in places and details that he hadn't covered.

As the dinner proceeded, the best and most current news came from Rebecca. She revealed that her high school grades and entrance exam scores had earned a scholarship to Berkeley. Because she had gotten word of this just that afternoon, she hadn't even had the opportunity to tell me before our dinner. She would study science at Berkeley and start in the fall.

"Do you plan to stay in the house, Miss Rebecca, while you go to Berkeley?" Alfredo asked, near the end of our dinner.

"I'm not sure," she answered.

I was a little saddened by the prospect of her leaving. The three of us—Rebecca, Alfredo, and I—plus Snappy, now getting old, had lived together in the house for eight years. If she moved, it would sort of mark the end of an era for our "little family."

Our waiter delivered desserts. Once he left, I glanced across the table at Rebecca. She looked sad, reflecting the way I felt at that moment.

"You okay, Sis?" I asked.

"I'm fine," she answered thoughtfully. "And this meal has been wonderful. But I was thinking . . .Only one thing could be better."

"What?"

"One of my mother's terrific spaghetti dinners," she smiled somberly. The rest of us nodded in agreement.

It turned out that Rebecca did continue to live in the house and commuted across the Bay Bridge to her classes at Berkeley. Predictably, she did very well there, especially in her science curriculum. In fact, she was the only undergraduate chosen for a select AIDS research team that met on campus most Tuesday afternoons.

Since she usually stayed after the meetings to compile or synthesize data, I usually cooked a late dinner for us Tuesday evenings. On one particular rainy November Tuesday night, I was in the house alone preparing our meal. Alfredo had gone out, and Snappy, having died of old age about a year before, was buried in our backyard, next to Dark Star, of course.

I looked out the kitchen window and saw the rain pelting down harder. As time passed, I became worried. We'd replaced Dad's old Buick with a newer car for Rebecca, but lately, it hadn't been running so well.

The phone rang, startling me. It was Alfredo, who informed me that he'd be back in a while with a friend. I suspected that the friend was a girl he'd introduced me to here at the house a couple of hours earlier. She surely wasn't the first girl he'd brought home. Truth was, over the years, I could only admire his wide array. None of them had ever come close to being permanent, though. Following break-ups, his standard comment was, "I like dogs better."

I returned to my cooking. Thunder kept sounding in the background. Finally, I heard the front door open, and I hurried into the living room. I was relieved to see Rebecca. She looked windblown, and the full-length raincoat she had on was wet. She dropped her umbrella into a bucket I'd put close to the door and hung her coat on a nearby rack.

"Glad you're home." I put an arm around her. "This weather . . ."

"It's fierce out there," she affirmed.

We walked into the kitchen. I could feel her shivering, so I turned on a space heater we kept there. After checking the food on the stove, I sat down with her at the kitchen table.

"I think we're on to something," she spoke enthusiastically. "At last, some of our trial and error is paying off."

"Your research team?" I questioned.

"Yes. Maybe a breakthrough. Consolidation."

"Consolidation?"

"We're trying to cut down on the number of medications by combining several," she explained. "Patients are taking too many now. At all times of the day and night. With all kinds of dangerous side effects possible. Chance of patient error is much too high."

I merely smiled. This wasn't the first time she'd discussed the research project with me, and I was sure it wouldn't be the last. Although I'd always tried to be supportive, I refrained from getting too involved in the technical aspects. Not because I didn't completely understand them, I simply wanted to remain an impartial observer. After all, I never had become entirely convinced that this commitment to AIDS was such a good idea for her.

"More news," she went on.

"About your research?"

"It's about my mother and our father."

"Oh?" I gulped a little, not expecting our dialogue to veer off like this.

"It's good news," she said. "They didn't get . . . sick from each other."

"Oh," I repeated my comment and the accompanying gulp.

"I checked their records."

"After all these years?" I asked, surprised. "You weren't even born when . . ."

"Yes," she interrupted, "but their records are clear. My mother had a different strain of the virus than Father. T-cell counts and dormancy periods prove they each had it when they first met."

Again I wanted to avoid technical aspects. So instead of replying, I got up to check our dinner on the stove once more. The vegetables I was steaming weren't ready. I sat back down.

"After I was born," she said, looking very serious, "do you think they ever went back to the stuff they were into . . . before?"

"What stuff?" I asked, my comfort level slipping further.

"You know . . . drugs and sex," she replied flatly, her tone subdued.

"How do you know about that?" My comfort level declined even more.

"My mother . . . I once overheard her talking to a friend. She spoke of the streets. I put two and two together. Anyway, how else would they have gotten the virus?"

I glanced anxiously at the stove, hoping to avoid her question. But I knew our food still wasn't ready. And I knew she had every right to know whatever I knew.

Certainly, I was aware of Dad's problems. And, over the years, Christina had revealed some of her past to me, too. As time went by, I couldn't help watching them both closely. I never saw the slightest hint that either of them might have lapsed into their former behaviors.

"No," I said firmly to Rebecca.

"No, what?"

"No, they never went back to the stuff they were into before you were born."

"Are you sure?'

"I'm sure."

"That makes me feel good," she said, looking relieved. "Like I was a positive influence."

"You were more than a positive influence," I responded quickly. "You were everything to them. You were their purpose in life."

She smiled at me and touched my hand. More thunder crackled, and we both glanced out the window. It was raining harder than at any time during the evening, and I wondered if Alfredo would be okay.

"Do you remember when I was young?" she asked. "When I had those symptoms?"

"Sure."

"And we went to the doctor? And he said it was nothing?"

"I remember."

"Well, he was wrong," she spoke decisively. "It was definitely something."

"Oh?" I was getting concerned that this was related to the disease, that somehow she'd become susceptible to it.

"Do you remember that reincarnation meeting?" she went on. "When I got real upset."

"Sure."

"That's when it first came to me."

"What did?"

"That's how my mother entered my body. How, in a way, I turned into her."

I'm sure I was more bewildered than surprised. To try to give me a little time to let this idea sink in, I decided to see if the vegetables were ready. I went to the stove, took the top off the steamer, picked up a fork, and stuck it into a carrot. Sure enough, it was tender.

"You must have resented it," I said, now more composed. "Your being . . . taken over."

"No. Quite the contrary."

"But it's not fair. Working on all those experiments. Trying to find a cure. It shouldn't be your burden."

"Maybe not," she replied. "But, like I gave her purpose, maybe she gave me mine. And anyway, I never had the chance to tell her . . . she's always been my hero. All she went through in her life."

I felt tears come to my eyes. I tried to focus on getting the food on the table. She got up to help me.

"I'd like to say something else," she spoke once more in a serious tone.

"What, Sis?"

"That you've been so much more than a big sister to me. Mother and Father, they couldn't have picked a better person . . . for me."

This time no question, my tears would follow. Luckily, the front door opened at that moment, and I heard Alfredo come into the house. He was laughing, and so was a female with him.

"I think Alfredo's got a new girlfriend," I managed.

"Another new one?" she chuckled.

"I met her earlier. You go in and say hello while I put the rest of dinner on the table."

Rebecca left the room. I could hear them chatting inside, and I was able to compose myself. Probably I'd become susceptible because Rebecca so rarely spoke of her feelings. By the time she returned, I had all our food on the table.

"What do you think of her?" I asked.

"She's very pretty."

"I agree."

"Not so sure that's in her best interest," she remarked.

"You mean," I replied, "instead of pretty, she'd have a better chance with him if she looked like a Dalmatian or a Collie."

We both laughed, then sat down to eat.

Epilogue

"She's always been my hero. All she's been through in her life."

Rebecca's words about Christina, spoken at the kitchen table that rainy night, often reverberated through my mind. Now, an evening a couple of years after that night, I thought of them again. I was sitting with Mother, Alfredo, and Lawson in an elegant conference room in a glamorous hotel. Years prior, Dad told me that this same hotel was ironically where he and Christina once went dancing before they were married.

The four of us were in an audience of about two hundred. We faced a small podium about fifty feet away, on which Rebecca and five others were seated. Above them hung a banner, "Bay Area Foundation for AIDS Research." An older man—tall, slender, tuxedoed—got up and stepped to the microphone at the front of the podium. When he spoke, his voice was deep, almost baritone.

"Thank you for joining us to honor this team of researchers seated behind me, for their very important contribution to the ongoing battle against AIDS."

I tried to listen to him, but instead, I kept hearing Rebecca's words on that rainy night. I was a first-hand witness to Christina's suffering in her final years. Also, she and Dad had said enough for me to realize she'd endured a lot before that, when her father's death sent her life into a tailspin. Apparently, her only good times after her early teens were those first years with Dad and with Rebecca.

Of course, I knew that Rebecca's words might apply to Dad as well. His last years were awful too. And there was no question that the loss of his former family—Mother, Stacy, and me—was very painful. In addition, I was certain that his compulsive nocturnal activities couldn't have ultimately been very satisfying.

"Our Bay Area Foundation," the speaker continued, "is proud to support not only local research to combat this dread disease but research throughout the country and throughout the world."

I glanced to my left at Mother, who flew in that day for the ceremony. I could tell by her rapt expression that she was happy to be here. As time passed, the frequency of her visits from L.A. increased to three or four a year. I often wondered what the proper terminology for her relationship to Rebecca was. Neither stepmother nor step-grandmother seemed to fit. Regardless, I was thankful for her involvement with Rebecca, who, after all, was Dad's daughter by another woman.

I was also thankful for Lawson. Since Dad's death, he always made himself available to Alfredo, very much like a father. And he'd done a terrific job overseeing our finances.

"Without the work of this fine team," the speaker said as he motioned behind him toward Rebecca and her associates, "it would continue to be extremely difficult for the average patient to maintain their medication regimen."

My gaze turned to Alfredo on my right. He looked quite handsome in his navy blue suit. I recalled Dad wearing a suit of the same color and texture two or three times. In fact, I remembered Dad giving Alfredo one like it—possibly this one—many years before.

Snappy came to mind. Especially how Alfredo saved his life. And then, almost as a way of showing gratitude, Snappy was so instrumental in rescuing Rebecca in her room that night she almost swallowed the chicken bone. The only time he ever barked during all the years he lived with us.

"By effectively combining certain medications," the speaker went on, "this team has greatly enhanced the entire treatment process."

As he continued, I glanced up at Rebecca on the podium. She had on a lovely red dress formerly Christina's, one that I'd never seen Rebecca wear before. She looked beautiful in it. I knew that, for sentimental reasons, it was Christina's favorite, and that she passed it on to Rebecca.

I thought back to the night Dad asked me to be Rebecca's guardian. I knew I had no regrets in accepting. Sure, I'd passed up the chance to start my own family. However, I had a wonderful family right here—Rebecca, Alfredo, Mother, and Lawson. Maybe I didn't have children of my own, but I'd certainly had the chance to play mother. And it had without question been fulfilling, especially with the uniqueness of my surrogate daughter, up there on the podium in that lovely red dress.

"I'm sure that eventually," the speaker announced, "there will be a complete cure for AIDS. In the meantime, thanks to major contributions like that of this research team, we keep making significant progress."

Loud applause echoed throughout the large room. I noticed that Rebecca shifted in her seat. I'd never observed her seeking any recognition at all for her work, and she seemed uncomfortable at the idea of receiving some now.

Again my thoughts spun back to Dad and Christina. About how they managed to find each other. And through their love, stopped surrendering to their addictions. About—to paraphrase Rebecca's words—all they went through in their lives. About how they never gave up, so that ultimately Rebecca could reach this moment.

The speaker introduced the members of the research project individually. Each stood up, and the audience applauded. When he got to Rebecca, he raised his voice and spoke more emphatically.

"And now, the leader of this wonderful team. Rebecca Stanton, please say a few words."

The audience applauded loudly. She had minimized her role with the group so much that I wasn't even aware she had been voted or appointed leader. That's how much she wanted no acclaim or personal attention for the work she was doing. As if the opportunity to do the work itself was all the reward she wanted.

As I watched Rebecca get up from her seat and step forward, I thought back to that afternoon when Christina and I sat at her kitchen table after I'd walked Rebecca home from her third-grade class. I thought back to how Christina had expressed the hope that maybe Rebecca could get things right for her. And now, as the moderator handed the microphone to Rebecca, I could see that that was exactly what had happened.

Rebecca had gotten things right for Christina.

About the Author

Alan Mindell's two novels (*The Closer*—2013, *The B Team*—2015) were published (not self-published) by Sunbury Press. *The Closer* has appeared on Amazon bestselling charts in four different categories. Both novels became Amazon's number one bestselling paperback in recently released sports fiction. Each is on Sunbury's all-time bestseller list.

A graduate of the University of California, Berkeley, he played varsity baseball for three years as a centerfielder. More recently, he coached high school baseball and basketball, and won numerous gold medals in San Diego's version of Senior Olympics. Out of this sports background, he wrote *The Closer*, a baseball love story.

He has owned and bred thoroughbred racehorses for many years, winning stakes at Del Mar and Hollywood Park. This experience prompted him to write *The B Team*, the story of a one-eyed horse who winds up in the Kentucky Derby.

He has written screenplays for both novels. He regularly teaches creative writing workshops at universities and other institutions and fulfills numerous speaking engagements throughout the greater San Diego area.

Made in the USA
Middletown, DE
21 January 2021